20p

Drift Raiders

Drift Raiders

DAN CLAYMAKER

A Black Horse Western

ROBERT HALE · LONDON

ISBN 0 7090 6464 0

Robert Hale Limited
Clerkenwell House
Clerkenwell Green
London EC1R 0HT

Photoset in North Wales by
Derek Doyle & Associates, Mold, Flintshire.
Printed and bound in Great Britain by
WBC Book Manufacturers Limited, Bridgend.

This for P.J.P. in appreciation
of his interest

One

Way beyond the frontier town of Duncan, and a hundred miles across the searing sprawl of the Blackcloud desert, lies the hell of the Drinkwater Drift, the only known fast passage west to the new territories of Colorado.

Given a full hand of luck, a keen eye for chance, some skilful mustering of resources and staying regular with the prayers, a man might just make it through that ungodly land and come out of it alive.

Takes guts and a grim determination to risk the Drift, and only a fellow with a real need to stay clear of searching eyes would gamble the odds. But many have and still do for whatever their dark reasons; folk of all shapes and sizes, from all sidewalks of life.

None more unlikely, though, than the couple who hit the Drinkwater in that high summer and, with no more than what they stood in and a hurriedly packed wagon, began the last leg of their long journey West.

7

Only they knew the hope of what they were heading to, and the dread of whatever they were running from. . . .

'Need to water up before noon,' said the woman, taking a hold against the creaking grind and bounce of the wagon, tightening her gaze against the sudden blaze of first light. 'Don't look hopeful.'

She glanced at the man seated in deep silence and concentration at her side. Sure, he had a guiding grip on the reins, the team under control over the rough, rock-strewn track; he had the *look* of a fellow given to the job in hand, but looks were about as far as it went, she thought.

His mind would be on other things, other times and another place way back – 200 miles back to be precise, to a dark night in a seemingly deserted street, to the shadowy shape of a stranger, a man whose name they had never known, who had died right there at their feet in the blaze and roar of gunfire.

'You hear me, Joe?' said the woman quietly. 'Water. We're goin' to need—'

'I hear yuh,' croaked the man, still watching the track. 'There'll be some.'

'I just hope you're right. All I can see is sand and rock. Goin' to be real hot come noon. Mebbe we should've held to the Blackcloud trail.'

'Too many folk. No place to hide.'

8

No, mused the woman, settling her gaze ahead, no place to hide. That was always Joe's priority these days: where was the next place to hide; where were the shadows deepest; where could he go and not be seen; where would the land swallow fastest? He would risk anything, even the Drinkwater, for a few hours of not having to look back to see who was following, who *might* be following.

She sighed behind a light cough and tightened her grip against another grinding bounce.

But for how much longer, she wondered, how many more sun-baked, scorching, dirt and dust-drenching miles? At the end of the Drinkwater, the frontiers of Colorado, the next town, a rundown homestead rotting in nowhere, or would they just keep going till the land ran out?

Warm, soft tears welled for a moment in the woman's eyes. She brushed them away hurriedly and settled her blurred gaze again.

If only there had been more time: more time to tell things as they had really happened, that the shooting had not been like it had seemed, to explain to Sheriff Marts that the man, whoever he was, had been there all night, watching them – watching her – and followed them when the wedding hoedown had broken up, been right there in their steps from the minute they had left the McLade home; following, staring, murmuring, only one thing on his mind. . . .

Of course she had seen the fellow – how could she have escaped that devouring gaze, the pale-blue eyes in the sweat-bright face that had, minute by minute, stare by stare, stripped every last stitch from her? And, of course, she should have said something to Joe right then, warned him, got away, just left.

But Joe had known, sure enough, oh, yes, he had known; felt that stare like it was on him, seen it through the party crowd, and maybe he had known what might be coming. Joe was no fool, not then, anyhow, and no man to tangle with neither when it came to some fellow getting a lathered up fancy for his wife.

But when it had finally happened. . . .

The man had been there, right there in the street, his hands reaching for her, almost finding a grip, and Joe had drawn his Colt maybe without thinking, instinctively, and loosed that one fatal shot. Just one miserly slug of lead.

And then no time at all. Only time to find Matt McLade getting them clear, urging them to pack, leave town, wait for the dust to settle, go anywhere, but just go, damn it!

They had, faster than they could think it, *without* thinking; hitching the wagon, throwing aboard what came to hand, whipping the team into the night, a deepening, sweat-soaked, haunted night. A night that had never ended. And they had brought their own ghosts.

They should never have done that, never run like they had. They should have stayed, faced Sheriff Marts, Judge Surface; explained, told it like it happened. Folk would have understood.

Or would they? Too late now. They had run, and once you were running. . . .

'Hawks circlin' to yuh left,' murmured Joe. 'Could be water.'

'Hope so,' smiled the woman softly. 'And lots of it! I need to wash and wash—'

'Goddamn it, Ellie,' snapped Joe, reining the team to a snorting halt, 'that all yuh can think of? Washin', f'Crissake!'

The woman braced herself against the jolt, sighed, brushed strands of loose hair into her neck, then stiffened, a tight, defiant line at her lips.

'Yes, Joe,' she said calmly, gazing ahead, 'right now that's all I can think of. Just washin'.'

'T'ain't a priority,' snorted Joe. 'Nothin' like it. And we ain't got the time.'

Ellie stiffened again and turned her gaze slowly to the man. 'Well, we're just goin' to have to make the time, aren't we?' She smiled, but the light in her eyes was already flaring.

'Hell, yuh just don't seem to get it into yuh head, do yuh; can't see it? Keepin' goin' is all that matters.'

'We been "keepin' goin'" for days, weeks, damn it! That's all we've ever been doin' – "keepin'

11

goin' ' ". Runnin', Joe, that's the truth of it. Just runnin', and no place to run to, 'til it's come to this, the hell of the Drinkwater!' Ellie shuddered as the words tumbled from her. 'Well, today's goin' to be different. Real different. Today, I'm goin' to wash – wash 'til I'm darned near all washed away! Yuh hear? And if that don't suit yuh "keepin' goin' ", yuh'll have to do just that, won't yuh – keep goin'. Alone.'

'Mebbe that's how yuh'd prefer it,' grunted Joe, twisting the reins through his fingers. 'Mebbe yuh'd be a whole lot better off alone. Get me right off yuh back, eh?'

'Oh, sure,' scoffed Ellie. 'Sure I would – that's why I been sittin' here gettin' a butt so sore it's on fire. That's why I been livin' off whatever half-dead game we could manage to shoot. That's why I been countin' the lead to see how many more rotten meals we got comin' up, measurin' out water like it was gold dust, wonderin' if I'm ever goin' to get outa this damned, stinkin' dress 'cus it's all I got and mebbe all I'm ever goin' to get; goin' near crazed outa my head on how we ever came to this, what happened to my home, my belongin's; lookin' back of me into this broken-down wagon at the bits and sticks we got that's supposed to be the future, and wonderin' what's happened to you, Joe Gates, and where and when and how in God's name all this is goin' to end.'

'Well, mebbe yuh should've thought a whole lot

12

more about that back at Duncan,' snapped Joe.

'And just what in hell's that supposed to mean?'

'Mebbe it weren't all that fella. Sure he was lookin' yuh over like he could eat yuh, but mebbe yuh were givin' him good reason to. Mebbe he had got to thinkin'—'

'That's about as darned fool-headed as yuh can get!' flared Ellie. 'Yuh think that? Yuh really think that? Yuh gettin' so twisted inside yuh to imagine for one minute I'd—'

Ellie's anger died in her throat and Joe's fingers stopped twisting at the sudden creak and groan of timbers, the bounce of tired wheels over rock behind them and the chilling realization that somebody, from somewhere, had found them.

TWO

He had the face of nightmares. A wet, rolling gaze that might have been liquor-hazed but deceived in the depth of its pierce; tight, parchment skin stretched to the limit over high cheekbones and a bulging forehead; a thin line of lips settled in a lopsided grin; stragglings of grey hair from beneath the black floppy hat; three weeks' stubble; trail dirt thick as cobwebs covering his clothes, and a voice that seemed to drift from nowhere.

'Howdy,' he called, reining his team to a halt, then raising an arm to steady the wagon following. 'Well, now,' he grinned, 'don't that Good Lord get to workin' in mysterious ways? Yessir, don't He just.' He patted the fat leather-bound Bible on the seat at his side, widened the grin over cracked teeth to a smile, lifted the hat with a flourish and bowed where he sat. 'Moses Ratrap at yuh service, folk, and real pleased me and my family'll be to make yuh acquaintance in this devil's wilderness. Yessir!'

14

'Don't say a word,' hissed Joe to Ellie from the corner of his mouth. 'I'll do the talkin'.'

Ellie stiffened, ran an anxious hand over sweating cheeks and narrowed her gaze on the man and the wagons.

Old, worn outfits that had done some travelling, she thought, and heavily laden with it – but not, she noted, against a sharp intake of breath, with household chattels and the trappings of trail-bound folk. Wherever Mr Ratrap had come from, wherever he was heading to, he had sure as hell been busy acquiring a 'family': a dozen rough-hewn, ragged men and a handful of tired-eyed women spilling from the wagons like flies from a bottle and clustering round Ratrap in a silent, staring swarm. Some family, mused Ellie.

'Meet the folk of the Good Word,' smiled Ratrap with a flourish. 'All God's children guardin' the ways of His word, spreadin' His message far and wide through a world fallen on evil times and the heathen core that breeds across it. Yessir, the messengers of the Good Word travellin' to the glory of the Lord.'

The man's eyes flashed and danced as he patted first the Bible then the head of a yellow-haired woman.

'Sure,' said Joe tentatively, shifting a boot cap through the dirt. 'Pleased to meet yuh . . . me and my wife here. Didn't reckon on meetin' folk trailin' the Drift. Figured we'd be—'

'Alone?' grinned Ratrap, leaning forward, a gleam in his narrowed gaze.

Joe swallowed and scuffed the boot uncomfortably. Ellie brushed strands of hair from her face and glanced hurriedly over the watching 'family'. Not a movement, not a murmur; only flat, waiting stares. She felt a sudden chill through the hazy morning heat and pulled nervously at the high neck of her worn, soiled dress.

'No man travels alone, mister,' said Ratrap, the grin slipping away, his hand settling again on the Bible, 'not while ever the Good Lord's ridin' with him. He back of that wagon of yours, friend?'

'We're headin' West,' said Ellie briskly, forcing a smile. 'Colorado. Makin' a fresh start. New life.' She was conscious of Joe stiffening at her side. 'Heard there's good land to be had out there.'

'Fresh start, eh?' Ratrap's grin snapped into place as if switched on. 'Well, now, you folk are in real luck. Yessir! The Lord is smilin' on yuh, 'cus it so happens that Colorado, the whole spread of God's glorious West, is the very destination of me and my family here. Yep, just so. We're Colorado bound, bringin' the Good Word to those brave, determined folk out there buildin' the future for all God's children.' He paused to wipe the back of his hand across his mouth. 'Least we can do, ain't it?' he added softly. 'Yeah, least we can do. . . . And you, I do declare, can travel right alongside of us, share the fortunes and the failin's of His bitter land we're crossin'. Join the family, be one of us. Yuh more than welcome, both of yuh.'

'Well, that's real nice of yuh, mister, and we appreciate—'

'Yuh wouldn't want to be slowed up by the likes of us,' said Ellie, cutting across Joe's murmurings. 'We don't travel fast, and we ain't in no hurry, and I'm sure yuh friends . . . yuh *family* here, ain't for draggin' out the miles, not in country like this.'

'My dear good lady,' smiled Ratrap, 'we are all of this one world, ain't we, all God's children in the cradle of His creation? Ain't no discriminatin' among us, ma'am. Nossir we share what we have, share and share alike, one for all and all for one in the name and love of our Lord.' The smile faded and the man's face darkened. 'Any case, this ain't no place for two folk to be travellin' like yuh are. T'ain't exactly the most wholesome place, 'specially not for a lone man and his woman, one wagon and a worn team. There's some here-abouts—'

'Some?' snapped Joe. 'Who?'

Ratrap leaned back and folded his arms. 'Tell 'em, Goose. Tell these good folk just how it is,' he grunted. 'Show 'em what we found.'

A tall, easy-moving, slow-eyed man stepped from the gathering, touched the brim of his hat and slid his weight to one foot. 'Apaches — maraudin' bunch of 'em circlin' these hills like hungry hornets, and they ain't in no mood to be

17

generous. Huntin' down all they can lay a hand to. Don't matter none. Anythin' movin' through the Drinkwater is game. We been lucky so far—'

'Good Lord's guidance,' interrupted Ratrap.

'Yeah,' said the man called Goose, with a glance at Ratrap, 'like he says. . . . And mebbe 'cus we're as many as we are. Them Apache ain't goin' to take us on in one raid, but they're sure as hellfire goin' to start pickin' us off 'til they figure we're weak enough for the full pluckin'.' He paused. 'Others ain't been so lucky.'

Goose nodded to a man at his side, took something from his outstretched hand and held the object high above his head. 'Seen one of these before, ma'am?' he asked, his gaze tight on Ellie. 'T'ain't a pretty sight, is it? Scalp, not two days old. Woman, about your age, I'd reckon. Near as damnit same shade of hair as yuh own. Came across it and a burned-out outfit back there on the trail.' He lowered the scalp and sighed. 'Wouldn't want to think of a good-lookin' woman like y'self comin' to an end like that.'

Ellie swallowed, stiffened and wiped a fresh gleam of chilled sweat from her cheek.

'Me neither,' croaked Joe brusquely. 'And it ain't goin' to happen, so me and Ellie here accept yuh offer, Mr Ratrap, and gladly. We'll be trailin' right along of yuh.'

'Now there speaks a man of sense and sound reasonin',' beamed Ratrap, unfolding his arms.

'Ain't that so, brothers and sisters?' The gathering murmured its agreement. 'Right, so let's flatten some of this Drinkwater dirt, shall we? Get these wagons rollin', eh? We got a whole clear day of trailin' comin' up. Good Word from the Good Lord! Here we come! Glory be! Hallelujah!'

'Hope yuh know what yuh doin', Joe Gates,' said Ellie a half-hour later when Joe had reined the outfit in behind Moses Ratrap's wagons and the teams moved off at a steady pace through the already sun-baked morning. 'Hope yuh thought this through.'

'Damnit, Ellie, 'course I have,' snapped Joe, his knuckles whitening in his grip on the reins. 'Don't yuh see it? Don't yuh see we suddenly got ourselves a perfect cover trailin' into new territory? Ain't nobody goin' to question Ratrap and his outfits, is there? They're goin' to see him for what he is – some Bible-punchin', hymn-singin' scat who ain't harmin' a soul savin' those he's goin' to wind up with his sermonizin'. And we stay close, nobody noticin', nobody givin' a damn, 'til we're good and ready to pull clear. First town we hit if we're lucky. And another thing: we ain't equipped for tanglin' with no Apache huntin' party. This way we stay alive and go free.'

'But, Joe—' began Ellie.

'But nothin'!' flared Joe, whipping the reins

across the team's backs. 'We stay with Ratrap, and that's it. Ain't no more to be said.'

Oh, but there is, thought Ellie, easing to the roll of the wagon. There was that scalp for a start. Three months old if it was a day, and no Apache worth his skin would leave behind a trophy at the site of a raid. As for scalping a woman . . . take her more like. And why had they not seen the burned-out outfit; at least caught a sight of the smoke? Hell, they had been on the same trail as Ratrap, only hours ahead of him.

And what about Ratrap and his so-called family? There was something awful strange about those women trailing with him. How come two of them had been splashed fit to choke with cheap eastern perfume? And how come they had all been wearing lace-trimmed pants beneath their short, bouncy skirts? Hardly the image of Bible-punching trail-busters!

And what about Ratrap; who was he, where did he hail from, and that fellow Goose at his side had all the looks of a gunslinger if ever she had seen one.

And how come nobody, it seemed, had spotted the lone rider who had been trailing high on the rim of the hills for the past hour? Was she the only one with eyes, damn it?

Three

They trailed hard and deep into the gritty dry beds, gullies and creeks of the Drift, the wagon timbers groaning with the effort, every bounce and splintering bump of wheels over rock echoing agony and ache, the teams snorting their protests, tossing their heads against the latherings of sweat and attacking flies.

But they were the only sounds through those first grinding hours. There was no place, and no incentive, for talk.

Ellie's silence, alongside that of husband Joe, seemed merely the cloak to the concentration of staying seated and the outfit on track. Only she knew and heard the turmoil of doubt, misgivings and now the first flickerings of fear raging through her mind.

How come, she was wondering, as wheels crunched over yet another fist of rock, that Ratrap and his followers were here at all? Why take to the Drinkwater when there were at least two

21

trails out of the Blackcloud desert that were easier, cooler and safer? Ratrap could have been preaching his way among the wagon-trains heading that way to his heart's content. So why the Drift? Only one reason, she reckoned – the same Joe had figured days back.

And that conclusion had chilled the sweat in her neck.

But were the same doubts and fears taking shape in Joe's thinking, she wondered? He was seated at her side, sweat-soaked, sunburned, steely-eyed, seemingly intent on the trail ahead and how to stay with it in one still rolling piece.

So maybe he was doing just that, she thought. Maybe he was content enough to hide behind the shield of Ratrap until they were safely across the border. Maybe that was the way: stay low, unnoticed, hidden in the folds of Moses Ratrap's 'family', let him figure how to stay clear of trouble, and how to deal with it if they did not. Could be Joe was seeing this as a change of luck, a better deal, a new hand and was going to play it for all it was worth. Could be he was right.

But supposing he was wrong. . . .

'He's gone,' said Ellie, shielding her eyes against the glare to scan the high rocky tops. 'Must've ridden on.'

'What?' croaked Joe, working the reins with the team's struggle. 'What yuh sayin'? Who's gone!'

'The rider. He was up there trailin' the ridge.

22

'Bout an hour back. Seemed to be followin' us.'

'Didn't see no rider,' groaned Joe.

'Mebbe yuh weren't lookin'.'

'Yuh seein' things. Sun's gettin' to yuh. Gets yuh like that out here.'

'No, I don't think so,' murmured Ellie. 'I saw him clear enough. He was there.'

Joe cracked the reins irritably. 'Yeah,' he muttered. 'You bet. Gettin' to see a whole lot of things, aren't yuh? Some rider nobody else's seen; some fella back at Duncan yuh reckon was—'

'Don't get back to that, Joe. Not now.'

'Right,' he snapped. 'So if yuh wanna go gazin', gaze for somethin' useful, will yuh, like them Apache sittin' on our butts.'

Ellie sighed and half-turned to watch the settling dust clouds behind them. Odd, she thought, how they seemed to hang there on the airless day like a curtain of mist. Fellow could trail in them for hours and never be seen.

'Now don't yuh go frettin' none, ma'am,' grinned Ratrap from behind the glow of the night's camp-fire. 'Yuh'll get used to the way of things round here. Takes time, and time we gotta deal of 'til we clear this godforsaken land.' He paused, blinked and smiled. 'Not godforsaken in that sense, yuh understand,' he added softly, his stare like a flame on Ellie's face. 'The Good Lord don't forsake

23

nothin'. Just gets to not givin' His full attention to some parts.'

He sipped carefully at the mug of hot coffee. 'See, we gotta simple way of doin' things as we spread the Good Word,' he went on, still smiling. 'Fellas do the drivin', the heavin' and the fendin'. Fightin' too if there's a need. Not that we encourage that, o'course. Then, come the end of the day, when the womenfolk have seen to the cookin', we get to relaxin', all of us, sorta meditatin' on the day's deliverance and the strength for those to come. Just like yuh fella there, talkin' with the boys and gals. Kinda peaceful and civilized, ain't it?'

Ellie shifted uneasily where she sat on the far side of the fire glow and pulled the dress tighter across her shoulders. Ratrap's stare was as disturbing as the slow drawl of his voice, but just about as monotonous, save for the edge that lurked around it.

'Come another day, ma'am, another twenty miles or so nearer our destination, good as the miles we've made today, and yuh'll be fittin' in just fine. Yeah, just fine. . . . Good thing we met up, eh? Yuh figure so?'

Now might be the time to mention Apaches, thought Ellie, to ask about that scalp, the burned-out wagon, why the 'family' were trailing the Drinkwater, and why it was the women here were. . . .

But perhaps not, she decided, finishing her coffee. No, not here, not yet, not this soon. Another day.

'As you say, Mr Ratrap, a good thing,' she smiled. 'We've made good progress, and I'm sure my husband and I are grateful to yuh. Perhaps I'd best join him. Time to turn in. It's been a long day.'

'Oh, no gratitude, please, ma'am. The Good Lord provideth. And no hurry neither. Boys get to talkin' real late.'

Ellie came to her feet slowly, smoothing her skirts as if freshly laundered. 'Even so—' She smiled again.

'Yuh travellin' light for settlin' folk,' said Ratrap, running his fingers round the coffee mug. 'Couldn't help but notice. Took a look in yuh wagon – beggin' yuh pardon. Just checkin', yuh understand.'

Ellie stiffened. 'Yuh had no right—' she began.

'All seemed a mite hurried,' said Ratrap without lifting his gaze from the mug. 'Now why would that be, ma'am? Yuh runnin' from somethin', somebody, by chance? That why yuh trailin' the Drinkwater? That why yuh ain't given me no name to call yuh by? That why yuh treatin' that dress like it's all yuh got? Mebbe it is, eh?' He lifted his gaze and grinned smoothly. 'None of my business, o'course, but if it's another dress yuh in need of, all yuh gotta do is slip outa that, ma'am, and I'll take care of the rest.'

Ellie's fingers moved through a line of sweat on her cheek and hovered like twigs shaking in a breeze. 'Thank you, I'll manage,' she murmured, and turned away from the glow to the night and the shadowy bulks of the brooding wagons – to anywhere that was beyond Moses Ratrap's suddenly devouring stare.

Ellie was still shaking when she reached the deepest shadows of the wagons. She brushed loose, damp hair from her cheeks, cleared the sweat at her brow, but shivered even so.

'Hell,' she murmured to herself, 'just what is all this?' and looked round her instinctively for Joe. She needed him right now; needed the touch of him, the closeness; needed him to tell her that this was not what she imagined, that she was mistaken, had got it all wrong, they had not stumbled into a rattlers' nest of deceit, crazed lust and maybe a whole lot worse.

But there was no Joe, not a whisper of him, nor was there likely to be, she thought, not while those scumbag 'boys' of Ratrap's 'family' were still into their relaxing, the so-called *meditating* that would sure as sun-up get to involving those sour-faced, scent-splashed girls before this night was a deal older.

She shivered again, hugged herself, and leaned back against a wagon wheel. This, the whole mangy set-up, was all wrong. Ratrap was no

26

Bible-punching evangelist, nothing close to it, and as for his *family* – hell, they were probably no more than a collection of drifters and gunslingers, just about every brand of loose-heeled vermin you could lay a name to. And those girls – no mistaking the cut of them. Any smoke-hazed, two-bit bar from here to the last point east would be home to them.

But that was hardly the point, was it, she mused, not the heart of it by a long shot? No, the point was, just what in hell's name were they doing here, trailing the Drift? Where were they going – and why and for what?

Ellie sighed, closed her eyes and eased to the silence of the night. Time to get a grip, she decided, get a hold of herself, start thinking clear. She needed to talk sense to Joe, get it into his head that if they stayed with Ratrap. . . . God knows what would happen if they did that. And she needed Joe to. . . .

No, damn it, she could see to that part of it herself.

She opened her eyes, stiffened, glanced round her and slid softly, silently, no more than a drift of shadow, to the rear of the wagon Ratrap had been driving. If there was anything at all that might be a clue to that crazed man's intent, then it would be there, in the back of his outfit.

All it needed was the guts to take a look.

Four

Ellie had a hand on the loose canvas flap at the back of the wagon before she had time to think twice. But then she paused, waited the few vital seconds to be certain she was alone, that the family was still relaxing and the dark shape of Ratrap still silhouetted against the fire glow; seconds of a brief uncertainty, and then fast resolve.

She had the wagon flap parted and had hoisted herself higher to see inside in one quick movement.

At first nothing, only a pitch darkness, shapes without shape, bulges, bundles, what might have been clothes, or just as easily a sleeping body; smells of sweat and spices, salted beef, whiskey – no mistaking the liquor – the dry tang of trail dust and dirt, but slowly, until it dominated all others, the smell of grease and fresh oilcloth.

It took barely a half-minute then for Ellie to locate the two wooden crates, for her fingers to slip over the lids, shift one the few inches needed for her hand to delve into the hidden depths and her touch to be sure, beyond any doubt, that wrapped in the oilcloth were rifles, Winchesters, greased and new and ready for use.

She swallowed a gasp, almost choked and was easing back to the night when the low croak of the voice behind her brought her to a frozen halt.

'What the hell . . ?' hissed Joe, grabbing her waist in both hands and pulling her clear of the wagon. 'Just what in God's name do yuh think yuh doin'? Yuh gone stark ravin' mad or somethin'?'

Ellie wiped her mouth, tossed her hair into her neck and stared hard and long into Joe's eyes. 'I'll tell yuh just what I'm doin', Joe Gates,' she croaked in little more than a cutting whisper. 'I'm rippin' this whole muck heap apart! That's what I'm doin'.' Her nostrils flared as the sweat gathered on her brow. 'Yuh know what's back there? Yuh got the remotest idea? Well, I'll tell yuh – rifles, Winchesters! Now just what, *in God's name*, do yuh figure our two-faced gospel-sharp is doin' with crates of brand-new Winchesters? We goin' on some turkey shoot, or is that how Mister-sin-buster-Ratrap converts the ungodly? He shoot 'em into prayer, Joe? That what he does? And while I'm diggin' in the dirt, it occurred to yuh to wonder how it is them girls of Ratrap's family are dressed like they are and smellin' fit to set a doghouse howlin'? Crib girls if ever I saw one, Joe

29

– or mebbe yuh found that out for y'self. Smells from here like yuh have! They come before or after the liquor? And as for that scalp—'

Joe Gates's swinging swipe at Ellie's face caught her clean across the cheek, sending her crashing across the wagon's wheel.

'Yuh outa yuh mind, woman?' he groaned, grabbing her shoulders. 'So help me, if I ain't lookin' at a sun-scorched crazy!'

'Go on, then,' moaned Ellie, slipping to the dirt, 'make a real job of it, eh? Finish it now, Joe. Go Bible-punch and shoot yuh way into Colorado, and take yuh pick of the calico queens with yuh! Why not! Yuh got 'em all here, ain't yuh?'

Joe was already tearing Ellie's dress from her when the hand settled like a rock on his shoulder and swung him round to face the searing glare of Goose.

'Boss wants to see yuh. Right now,' grinned the man, levelling a steady Colt as he stepped back. 'Call to prayer, yuh might say!'

Ellie crawled on all-fours through the dirt in the steps of Goose and Joe, her dress hanging from her bare shoulders like a loose rag, sweat plastering her hair to aching flesh, eyes as round and dancing as wild moons, her mind in a spinning turmoil. Suddenly the night, the granite-stiff shadows and stifling darkness, were closing in, suffocating, pressing her to the still baked earth.

She followed Goose's crunching boots, Joe's

slithering steps at gunpoint until they merged with a forest of legs – Ratrap's men, the bare-legged girls in the flouncing – skirts and came slowly, painfully upright when Goose finally pushed Joe ahead of him, into the piercing, gleaming stare of Ratrap seated at the head of his outfit, one hand flat as a stone on his Bible.

'Well, now, friend,' smiled Ratrap, leaning forward to fix the stare tight on Joe's face, 'ain't you just been a busy fella?'

'All I was doin'—' spluttered Joe.

'Oh, sure, sure, we know what yuh were *doin'* friend, that's the easy bit. But that ain't it, is it? Nossir. Its *why* yuh were probin' around back of my wagon. My wagon! In the Good Lord's name, fella, yuh sure try a man's patience comin' to that.'

'Yuh got it all wrong, Mr Ratrap,' protested Joe. 'When I got here I found—'

'And we all know what yuh *found*, don't we?' snapped Ratrap. 'That don't take no figurin' neither. Trouble is, mister, yuh ain't no part of what yuh found back there. No part at all. Yuh see, them rifles yuh found – oh, now, don't look so surprised, mister, we know yuh seen 'em – them rifles are a kinda investment. Ain't that so, boys and gals?'

The gathering murmured.

'Yeah,' grinned Ratrap, 'all part of our future – the glory comin' up.'

31

'Well, that's fine by me,' shrugged Joe. 'I ain't plannin' on interferin' none.'

'Yuh right there, fella,' sneered Ratrap. 'Dead right.'

'Far as I'm concerned,' Joe shrugged again, 'man's entitled to do as he pleases, go as he pleases. T'ain't none of my business.'

'Well, now, I gotta be real sure about that.'

'Yuh can be sure, Mr Ratrap,' smiled Joe. 'Real sure. Yuh been good enough to take us in, and once we're clear of the Drift—'

'Oh, my,' groaned Ratrap, pushing aside the brim of his floppy hat and raising his eyes to the night sky. 'I feel a Judas among us, friends. Oh, yes, I feel a Judas right there.'

'Judas! Judas!' echoed the followers.

'Hey, now, hold on, will yuh?' croaked Joe.

'Judas! Judas!'

Ellie squirmed her way through the gathering. 'It was me!' she shrieked. 'Me. I was the one—'

'Stay outa this lady,' snapped Goose, dragging Ellie to him.

'I can't abide a Judas,' leered Ratrap. 'No place, no time.' He lowered his gaze to Joe's sweating face. 'Let's see what the Good Book says, shall we? Seek our guidance here.'

Ratrap's fingers crawled slowly over the cover of the Bible, paused, lifted the cover, paused again. 'Ah, yes,' he murmured. 'Of course. . . .'

Ratrap had reached into the box beneath the

Bible cover, drawn the Colt and fired a blaze of shots into Joe Gates's throat and chest before anyone had blinked, before the gasp and then the scream had cleared Ellie's mouth, and long before the night, the faces of the gathering, the shadowy shapes of their bodies and the haunted gloom of the Drinkwater Drift had tumbled to a swimming haze across her eyes and she collapsed in the dirt, unconscious.

'That woman needs a new dress,' croaked Ratrap.

Five

Marshal Sam Cavendish reined the black mare to a halt just short of the steep, winding track to the gully, eased her into the shadows and dismounted, as grateful as the horse to relish for a while the depths of cooler shade.

He slung his canteen free, poured water into the cup of his hand and nuzzled it at the mount's mouth. 'Easy, gal,' he murmured. 'Short supplies 'til we reach the Claw.'

He waited until the mare had snorted her satisfaction, flicked her ears at his gentle patting, then stood back, took a single gulp from the canteen, rolled the tepid water round his throat and spat it out to a sizzling black stain at his feet. He sighed, corked the canteen and slung it back to the saddle.

Time for another check, he thought, drawing his Winchester from its scabbard and scrambling awkwardly into the sprawl of sun-baked boulders.

Barely two hours after first light and already

34

the Drift was a shimmering cauldron of scorched dirt and clinging dust. No place for man or beast, he reckoned, save men too spooked to care and beast too crazed to worry. Not that Moses Ratrap had ever been spooked, or even close to it. Ratrap knew no fear, not with his twisted belief in the God-almighty of his own making, and had never run or turned his back on anything. But he had 'led' his ragbag scum into the Drinkwater, and that was a puzzle. That was out of character – or another side of the fellow Cavendish had never seen in the year he had been sitting on his tail waiting for the sonofabitch to make a false move.

Yessir, Ratrap taking to the Drift was indeed a puzzle and close on two weeks of trailing him out of the eastern plains had yielded nothing remotely like an explanation of why he was here, with the family at full strength, where he was heading or for what purpose.

Cavendish grunted hoarsely, swallowed on his dirt-sore throat and licked quickly at the salty sweat trickling to his lips.

No such problem with that fool couple high-tailing it out of Duncan. They were spooked to the core, running scared and dragging their fear with them in chains, had to be, could only be, to take this route off the Blackcloud. Pity of it was he had been only hours from catching up with them, just as he had promised Sheriff Marts he would, when Ratrap had hit their trail.

And that, sure as hell, *had* created a problem. What to do: get to the couple and reveal himself to Ratrap, or sit back, trail on, and leave them to whatever their fate with the infamous family?

He had gambled on the couple's luck changing, and not slept a wink since. Now, it might already be too late. Ratrap had no credentials for being kindly, let alone patient, especially where a good-looking woman was concerned.

Damn it, he cursed through his thoughts, he should have looked to the woman first and left Ratrap to some other arm of the law. Trouble with that reckoning was that he wanted Ratrap more, right now, than he wanted water, would even give what little he had bottom of his canteen to get his hands on the Bible-punching rat.

He grunted again, swallowed on the same dirt-sore throat. Best face it, admit it, Moses Ratrap haunted him. But how close in twelve months of snapping at the fellow's tail had he come to haunting Ratrap? Well, maybe not close enough, but he was still here, still following, ahead of him now, waiting, watching for that one false move. And when it came. . . .

He eased a foot higher for a wider view at the sound of creaking timbers, groaning wheels. Here they were, right on time, same place, same pattern, Ratrap's wagon leading, Goose Farrars in the outfit following, the couple's wagon bringing up the rear.

The marshal narrowed his eyes, tightened his gaze. Neither Joe Gates nor his wife were at the reins. So what, why. . . ? The gunshots he had heard after dark, had they been more than liquored high-jinks? Hell, had Ratrap got to. . . .

Sam Cavendish slid from the boulders to the dirt with a gut-twisting sigh and a sudden lathering of cold sweat, and was still sweating when he mounted up and swung the black mare back to the sunlit track to the Drift.

Ellie Gates thought she knew now just what Hell really looked like; she knew the shape of it, the smell of it, could reach out and touch it, and was as sure as she had ever been of anything that once into it there was no escape.

Hell was the back of Moses Ratrap's wagon, waking from a stunned, nightmarish sleep to find yourself in it among the stinking clothes and trappings of a crazed man's life, crates of rifles tight at your back, the shadows watching you, and right there, black as some fixed storm cloud, the shape of the man driving the outfit who, not hours back, had shot your husband in cold blood while you could only stand and watch.

That was the making of Hell.

She swayed to the monotonous pitch and roll of the wagon, pulled the torn dress across her shoulders, wiped the sticky sweat from her cheeks and neck, closed her eyes and drifted once again into a swirling jumble of sounds and images. . . .

They had thrown Joe's body aside and the family gathering dispersed back to the fire and liquor when she had come to, leaving only Ratrap watching her from his perch on the wagon, one hand on the Bible box, a soft grin at his lips. She had stared in silence into the man's face for a full dark minute, drained then, it seemed, of all emotion, without fear, remorse or anger, cold and emptied.

Maybe she should have turned then and run, kept running, deep into the night, until she plunged either to a wilderness of certain death or Ratrap shot her in the back. No matter, she had been staring death in the face ever since that night in the street at Duncan. And now, with Joe gone. . . .

Why were there no tears, she wondered, no consuming grief at her loss? Too soon, or too late? Had Joe's distrust, the twisted suspicions and doubts finally broken their love? Did it matter now? They had been trailing to an end the minute they had climbed aboard their wagon and left town. There would never have been any going back, anyhow. The end was coming soon enough. Only question now was, who would lay first claim, the Drift or Ratrap?

Right then, she had thought it might be Ratrap, but he had shown no further interest in her — simply packed her like so much baggage into the back of his wagon and posted a guard – and right now, bounding and bumping their slow way through the first light of another scorching day, she would favour the Drift.

Ratrap would have to water up soon, she reckoned, and that might mean breaking the trail. Nor did it seem to Ellie that the outfits were making the progress he intended. Did he have a timetable? Did they have to be wherever they were going for whatever purpose at a certain time on a certain day?

And why, since the shooting of Joe, had Ratrap started to look a deal more shifty-eyed? Was he concerned that someone might be following? The rider she had seen high on the hills? And, come to think of it, where was he, *who* was he? A drifter who had simply drifted on? Somebody looking out for Joe Gates – too late now! – or somebody trailing in Ratrap's shadow?

Or maybe there was a whole new concern troubling the fake Bible-puncher.

'Steady 'em up there, Goose,' yelled Ratrap suddenly, reining the outfit to a grinding halt. 'Dust cloud half-mile on. Riders coming in fast. Get the boys loaded up and them gals outa sight. Any curiosity, we shoot first and keep just one alive. Wanna know who they are and where they're from. Got it?'

Ratrap half-turned in his seat to stare into the wagon at Ellie. 'And you, lady, stay real quiet, eh?

Not a murmur, unless yuh want me to stitch them juicy lips tight shut.' He grinned as his eyes began to gleam. 'And get y'self covered up some. Yuh supposed to be a grievin' widow, f'Crissake!'

Six

It was another five minutes before the cloud was close enough to take on the dark blurs of recognizable shapes. At least a dozen riders, thought Ellie, shifting to left and right for a clear view from the back of the wagon over Ratrap's shoulder. Fast, hard-riding men who were either putting scorched dirt between themselves and something way behind, or in one hell of a hurry to reach the wagons, and even at this distance as grisly a bunch as you would go some way to avoid.

Ellie shivered at Ratrap's shouted orders to Goose in the wagon drawn up alongside him.

'Heathen-lookin', ain't they? Not a calm soul among 'em, you bet. Barren hearts ripe for reconciliation with their Maker, Goose. Oh, yes,' he grinned, 'fellas in sore need of solace and comfort, wouldn't yuh say? Yuh all set? The boys ready?'

'Ready,' called Goose.

'That's good, very good,' murmured Ratrap, beginning to hum, his fingers drumming lightly

41

on the Bible box, eyes gleaming. 'Yuh just stay low there, lady,' he croaked between the tuneless litany. 'Don't want that pretty head of yours harmed in no way. Nossir! Got a whole future mapped out for you. And how!'

Ellie shivered again through a surge of cold sweat and wondered for one crazy moment if she might grab one of the Winchesters crated right there at her side, rummage for some ammunition and blast a hole the size of a fist through Ratrap's head. Some hope. She had never fired a Winchester in her life, and now was no time to start taking lessons! All she could do was watch and wait – and maybe pray.

The leading rider reined tight some distance short of the wagons, sat easy while the dust cleared and his companions joined him, then casually lit a cheroot and scanned the outfits like a hawk through the drifting smoke.

'You folk Colorado bound?' he drawled, aiming a line of spittle deep into the sand.

'By the Grace of the Good Lord,' smiled Ratrap. 'Given His blessin'.'

The man chewed hungrily on the cheroot, his gaze rooting into Ratrap's face. 'Sun-busters,' he croaked, nodding to a rider at his side.

'Spreadin' the Good Word, my friend,' said Ratrap, pushing at the brim of his floppy hat. 'Oh, yes, indeed, sowin' where the land is cruel for the riches of the Lord's harvest.' His smile broadened.

'And y'selves, sir? Headin' East?'

The man blew more smoke. 'Ain't fussed. Anywheres there's pickin's.'

Ratrap's fingers began to drum on the Bible box. 'Pickin's, eh – well, we sure cross them often enough. Yessir. Flotsam of our sins, my friends. Flotsam. But that ain't to say—'

'What's back of yuh wagons?' snapped the man, reining his pawing mount.

'Why, no more than yuh'd expect,' smiled Ratrap. 'The basics of our lives, sir. This and that and never more than needed. T'ain't in our nature to take upon us the grander materials of life. Ain't necessary. Ain't needed. Man don't need more than—'

'We'll see for ourselves,' snapped the man again.

'Well, now,' said Ratrap slowly, 'yuh more than welcome to share what we have, friend. Food and what little water we have. Does a man a power of good to share what the Good Lord bestoweth, but I ain't so sure about—'

'Sharin' ain't what I got in mind,' clipped the man, wafting a hand through a thicker cloud of smoke as the riders eased closer to him. 'I'm for takin'. Regular religion with me, ain't it, boys?'

The riders tittered and slapped at hot leather.

'That so?' said Ratrap softly, beginning to hum. 'That a fact? Takin', eh? Yuh mean helpin' y'selves?'

43

'Just that. Exactly that.'

Ratrap fell silent, his fingers still and bent on the box. 'Don't go along with robbin'. Never have. It's a mangy, gutless occupation in a grown man, don't yuh reckon? Lacks pride, yuh see, and a fella without his pride . . . well, he ain't worth a spit, is he? Now me – Moses Ratrap at yuh service – me, I'm all for handlin' things different. Seekin' the word of the Lord, seein' what He has to say right here in the Good Book. . . .'

Ellie stiffened in the chill of her sweat at the sight of Ratrap's fingers coming back to life on the fake Bible cover. They began to drum, at first lightly, delicately, like the patter of soft rain; paused, one finger bent above the others; drummed again, willing the gaze of the riders into watching as if suddenly hypnotized by the rhythmic sound, the steady movement.

This was it, she thought, Ratrap's coded message being tapped out to the family. This was the way he 'spoke' to them, told them what was coming and when. Every man, every woman back of his wagons would be alerted, concentrated on the pattern of sound, 'reading' it as clearly as they might listen to his spoken word.

Ratrap had no need to say anything, he was saying it all right there on the cover. And when the drumming stopped, when those scumbags were simply sitting transfixed, waiting for the fingers to lift, the sound to return, then they

44

would snap like a claw, raise the cover and reach for the Colt.

And the gates of Hell would swing wide open.

She swallowed and began to ease back slowly to the rear of the wagon. Was it a chance, or a wild bid in desperation to think that in the mayhem that was about to erupt she might escape? Could she get clear of the wagon, make a run for it?

But to where, damn it?

She risked as quick a glance through the back-flap as she dared. Sand, dirt, loose rock, faint outcrops, but the outfits had halted closer to the hills than she had thought.

Close enough to make a dash for them?

She eased back again, stiff with tension, soaked through now with hot, running sweat. Hell, it was some distance to cover, she thought. Did she have the strength, the stamina for it? Any one of the guns that would soon be blazing might seek her out, spill lead into her back. But even if she made it, what would she be running to?

Death – as simple and uncomplicated as just that. Well, if that was going to be the way of it, least she could do was give herself some choice. Ratrap or the hills?

The hills, any time, any day!

The spit and roar of firing, sudden yells, wild shouts, screams and curses, thrust Ellie back to reality with a jolt. She bit nervously at her lower lip, closed her eyes for a moment on the swirling dust clouds, her ears against the roaring madness, ran shaking fingers down her sweat-streaked cheeks, and then, fully alive again but shivering almost beyond control, swung herself from the wagon to the dirt and began to run, skirts flying across her thighs, the dress no more now than a shredded rag.

She heaved, gulped for every stabbing breath from the burning air, worked her legs until she thought they might snap like bone-dry twigs, and saw nothing save the blurred haven of the distant hills.

Or the hell of them.

Damn it, the fool woman was making a run for it! She would never make it – never, not like that, not out there.

Sam Cavendish struggled higher, to the very rim of the crags, until his head and shoulders were fully exposed in the shimmering blaze of the sun.

Just what in God's name was the woman thinking of, he cursed, through a hissing intake of breath? If Ratrap's guns missed her, the drifters would take her out like swatting a lame fly. It was madness, suicidal – that precisely, *suicide*.

Maybe she had reached that point; maybe death in the rage of hot lead was a sweet alternative to a mauling at the hands of Ratrap. If it was a harsh fact now – and it sure as hell looked like it – that Ellie Gates's husband was dead, then running for whatever slender grip on life the woman had was about all that was left to her.

Cavendish drew his Winchester alongside him. Could be he was just close enough to fire a hail of diverting gunfire, draw the blazing shots at the wagons away from the woman, give the scum another target. Or would he be slinging his neck into the very noose he wanted to avoid, had spent these past days guarding so carefully against? One hint of shots from the hills and Ratrap would need no more than two fingers to work out the odds of just who was doing the firing.

Or should he get closer, maybe sneak out to that outcrop, attract the woman to him and just hope. . . ? Hell, no, that way they would both be crow meat come sundown.

He shifted his gaze to the wagons. Ratrap had the upper hand there, no doubt about it. Another few minutes and the bushwhackers out of nowhere would have bushwhacked their last.

But what about that fool woman?

She was still running, weaving to left and right, the torn dress flowing from her body like wisps of dark cloud, her legs lost in the swirling dirt, hair flowing from her neck. But there was no mistaking the shots winging round her. Ratrap had spotted her, sure enough, and was doing his darnedest to make sure she bit dirt fast.

Only a matter of time now before somebody's

aim proved good, downed her, maybe – if she was that unlucky – just wounded.

Hell, this was madness! Just what in the name of decency did he think he was doing sprawled here like some sun-fazed lizard waiting for the shade? Move, damn you, do something.

And in the next moment Marshal Sam Cavendish had slid out of cover and was spitting hot sand.

Seven

Moses Ratrap stood in a cloud of drifting smoke and dirt and stared into the parched, scorching sprawl of the Drinkwater Drift without blinking.

Some might have thought he was thinking, deep in a contemplation of remorse for the dozen or more blood-soaked, twisted bodies around him. Some might have generously figured him for offering the last rites, dispatching as was fitting those for whom the struggle for survival had taken the ultimate toll. Some might even have reckoned him for being in a state of genuine grief for those he had personally put to the bullet.

They would all have been wrong.

Moses Ratrap was, in fact, reaching the boiling point of his anger, twitching with the surges of sweat that surfaced like tides across his skin, working his wet fingers constantly through clawing twists and stretches as if rehearsing a strangulation.

That woman, damn her, had gotten free, and no woman, tart or duchess, did that to Moses without paying her due. And she would, oh, yes, she surely would, just as soon as that goddamn sun up there had near burned her to a cinder and she would give her life for a spit of water.

Soon, very soon, he reckoned, long before sundown she would come crawling out of them dirt hills like a gut-drained hound, pleading for water, and Moses, feeling fellow that he was, would give it to her, just enough to bring her round, keep her alive, while he made a sun-baked, waterless day seem like a heaven compared with the hell of night.

'Yeah,' he murmured, then turned quickly. The anger passed, the wagons, the family, Goose, dead bodies and the future in need of his attention.

'Get this mess cleaned up and let's pull out,' he scowled, as Goose and a group of the men approached. 'Can't stand mess no how.' He pushed irritably at the floppy hat. 'We all in one piece? Any losses?'

'Scratches,' said Goose. 'We took most of them scum out before they could blink – savin' one. He's still breathin'.'

'He say much?'

'Enough. Seems like the fella leadin' the bunch had brought 'em up from the south. Drifters, the whole pack. Headin' out to the main trail off the Blackcloud for what they could take. Stumbled into the Drift by mistake. Figured us for an easy pickin'.' Goose grinned. 'Some mistake, eh?'

'Big as they come!' smiled Ratrap, then, through another scowl, 'Finish him. And make it quiet. No more shootin'.'

Goose grunted. 'What about the woman? We goin' after her?'

'No,' snapped Ratrap. 'She'll be crawlin' out of them hills before sundown. We'll pick her up when we're good and ready.' He pushed at the hat again. 'How long before we hit Eldron?'

'Four days. Right on time by my reckonin'.'

'Hmmm,' grunted Ratrap, scratching at an armpit. 'Don't want no more diversions. We water up at the Claw t'night, then push straight on. Tell the gals to share themselves out come sundown. Boys can have a party. They earned it.' He turned to squint at the shimmering heat-haze over the hills. 'I just sometimes get the strangest feelin' . . .' he murmured.

'We ain't bein' trailed,' said Goose. 'Stake my life on it. Them Apache we spotted must've drifted on.'

'T'ain't Apache that bother me. It's an itch, right there between my shoulders, and when I get to itchin'—'

'Yuh scratch real vicious!' laughed Goose. 'We seen it! Well, yuh got no need to fret, Moses, there ain't a soul out there save for that fool woman, and she ain't nobody.'

Ratrap grunted but continued to stare. Not everything Goose said could be taken as gospel.

Plain crazy, or plain stubborn; black or white, not a spit of grey to be seen, so you took your choice with a woman like Ellie Gates and hoped for the best. But either way, you would be stringing yourself out on a hiding to nothing and trying to look brave.

Sam Cavendish was finding it awful hard to look anything like brave.

He shifted his feet through the dirt on the far side of the shade, leaned back on the rock, sighed, mopped the sweat from his brow and watched the woman where she dozed fitfully in the deep shadow.

Say one thing for her, though, he thought, brushing aside a persistent fly, she recovered fast, seemed to shrug off ache and exhaustion without a pinch of effort. Or was that all some part of the act?

No, he reckoned not. That had been no mask of fear on her face when he had finally scrambled to her side at the outcrop and began to drag her out of gunshot range into the hills. Nor had she been acting out those shudders, the shivering that had racked her whole body, and those cuts and bruises were no fancy make-up.

No mistaking either the look of despair at Cavendish's first touch, the relief when he had explained who he was and why he was out here and that, if they kept their heads, stayed low awhile, chances were Ratrap and his wagons would roll on.

She had drunk nervously but gratefully from the marshal's canteen while he had watched the action in the Drift, and waited till the hills were silent again and the air heavy with the pungent smell of cordite before beginning to explain who she was, how she and her husband had fallen foul of Ratrap, of her discovery of the crated Winchesters, the shooting of Joe, but nothing, not a hint, of the events of the fateful night in Duncan.

It had taken Cavendish all the guts he could summon right then to come to the brutal point.

'Yeah,' he had murmured slowly, 'most of what yuh've told me I knew, ma'am, savin' about them Winchesters. I got to sittin' on yuh tail soon after yuh hit the Drinkwater.'

'I saw yuh,' Ellie had smiled, 'just knew I had. Said as much to Joe.'

'And nobody else, I hope.'

'Nobody.' She had waited a moment as if sifting the shapes of jumbled thoughts. 'Yuh seem to be sayin'—' she had begun again.

'I'm sayin', ma'am, as how I knew who yuh were, where yuh'd come from – and why – and if it hadn't been for Ratrap hittin' the Drift—'

'You passed through Duncan?' Ellie had

croaked through a new shudder. 'You knew—?'

'I knew. Headed into town not so long after yuh'd pulled out. Checkin' with Sheriff Marts there on Ratrap. Heard the whole story.'

'The *whole* story, Mr Cavendish?'

The marshal had stared long and hard into Ellie Gates's face at that point, had traced every line of the hardship, fear and agony of the trek, the fear that had ridden with her like a shadow, the cold, bewildering death of Joe, and now the uncertainty as she sat, broken and lost, face to face with the law.

'Yuh husband gunned a fella,' he began.

'But it wasn't just like that—' Ellie had said sharply.

'Fella's name was Bart Shipley, driftin' gunslinger, just happened into town that night, stood alongside the weddin' hoedown for no better reason than it was there. Point is, Mrs Gates, Shipley was wanted through a half-dozen territories on counts of rustlin', robbery, murder – and rape. There was a price on his head. *Dead or alive.*'

It had taken seemingly endless minutes for Ellie's flat, unblinking gaze to swim into focus again and her cracked, dry voice to break the silence.

'So Joe didn't commit no murder. He wouldn't have hanged, not no how,' she had croaked. 'There'd been no need to leave. If we'd waited for Sheriff Marts, told him how it was. . . . It was all a waste, a terrible, terrible, waste. . . .'

Cavendish had stayed silent as Ellie had come unsteadily to her feet and turned her back on him. There had been tears in her eyes, sure enough; a new agony now, of futility, waste, the loss of a life, the cold-blooded shooting of her man for no good reason. And perhaps the grim reality beginning to dawn of a future that was about as gritty, burned out and useless as the dirt across the Drinkwater Drift.

Maybe he should say something, anything, just fill the space with sound, he had thought, tell her that somehow, in some way, he would get her back to Duncan, her home and roots, just as soon as that scumbag, Ratrap, out there made his next move.

'Those rifles, Mr Cavendish,' the woman had said firmly, her back still to the marshal, 'in the wagons – how do you suppose Ratrap plans to use them?'

'No sayin', ma'am. Never is with him. Could be he plans on sellin' 'em, tradin' 'em, or mebbe he's—'

'Be useful if yuh knew, wouldn't it?'

'Sure it would, but that's for me to figure, ma'am. Thing now is to get you safely outa here.'

'Trouble is yuh can't get close enough to find out, can yuh, not without him knowin' you're sittin' on his butt?'

'That *is* the problem, ma'am.' Cavendish had

shrugged, with a quiet grin to himself. 'But there's mebbe a chance—'

'No, Mr Cavendish, there's better than a chance. There's a way.'

Ellie Gates had turned slowly, her eyes sharp and bright through the skimming of shade that crossed her face, her arms stiff and straight at her side, the dress hanging from her like a draping of weeds. Her voice now was steady, levelled and matter of fact.

'You can't get close to Ratrap, Marshal, but I can.'

'Damn it, ma'am,' Cavendish had groaned, 'yuh couldn't even begin to think—'

'I'm all through with thinkin', Mr Cavendish. I done enough of that these past weeks to last a lifetime. Time's come for doin', and gettin' to it.'

'Hell, if yuh goin' to suggest what I think's rattlin' round yuh head, ma'am, yuh plain—'

'Crazy? Well, mebbe so, but crazy folk do the craziest things, don't they, and it's 'cus they're so crazy they sometimes work.' Ellie had taken a long, deep breath. Cavendish had groaned and closed his eyes in despair. 'Now, you listen, Marshal, and listen good. Ratrap needs to water up, right? Right, so wherever that's goin' to be is where I'm goin' to be, waitin' on him, smilin' a big warm welcome.'

'He'll shoot yuh minute he sets eyes on yuh. Or worse, he won't!'

'No, Mr Cavendish, yuh wrong. I know exactly what Moses Ratrap will do.'

'Yuh really don't know him at all, ma'am,' the marshal had scoffed.

'Mebbe a deal better than yuh think. In case yuh f'gotten, I'm a woman. Anyhow, I can handle that. Main thing is to find out what Ratrap's plannin' with them Winchesters, when and where.'

'Yuh think he's goin' to tell yuh, just like that?'

'He'll tell me. Don't yuh doubt it.' Ellie had pulled the dress across her shoulders with a sudden tug. 'Meantime, Mr Cavendish, you'll be stayin' close, outa sight, but close. There'll be a message left on the trail for you every night. Make sure yuh find it! And once we're certain of Ratrap's plan, yuh'll move ahead – go wherever yuh need to be and arrange a suitable reception! You'll have as much time as I can give yuh. Right? Yuh got that?'

'If you think I'm goin' to let yuh—' Cavendish had begun.

'This is my show from here on, Marshal. Mine all the way. Yuh need me for what I'm plannin', and don't say yuh don't. Yuh'd be lyin'. And I need . . . well, that's my affair. Mebbe yuh can figure it for y'self. Right now, we're wastin' time and breath. Give me however long we can spare to rest up, then get me to where them wagons are goin' to be come sundown. Get me to Ratrap!'

Plain crazy, or plain stubborn, Cavendish

mused again, shielding his eyes against the sun's glare as he reckoned the hours to dusk. But far from being plain dumb. Nossir, nothing like.

Even so, the sweat in his neck was running ice-cold when he finally moved to wake the woman.

Eight

Moses Ratrap was watching the thickening shadows as if expecting any one of them to suddenly move, slip across the dirt to the slow rolling wagon and spit clean in his eye.

There was not a single one out there to be trusted. They were the dark, brooding enemy and not to be given an inch. He would shoot the first black devil that so much as shifted. So he would at that, damn them!

His fingers curled in their grip on the reins where they rested easy on the team's backs. Still, he pondered, no need to hurry, no need at all. Time was a cool partner right here at his side. No fretting, no panic. They would be at the Claw and watering-up well before nightfall. Party time, some relaxation for the boys and girls before the final two days' push to Eldron. And then. . . . Well, now, that was where the future would be sitting up and taking notice. Yessir!

Only one thing fidgeted him, niggled like a loose burr slipping round a boot.

That woman. Damn it, she haunted fit to chill; never seemed more than a spit from his thoughts. Sure, she had made a run for it, got clear away to the hills – he would hardly have reckoned her for anything less – and sure as feathers in a mattress she would be back, dehydrated as a twig, but that was not the fidget.

No, it was just something about her, something in her eyes that had come with widow's weeds. Something he had seen before, many times in the eyes of many men – long Boot Hill settled now – but never in a woman.

So what had she figured on seeing them rifles? What *could* she figure? Rifles were rifles and had no voice. They had told her nothing, but they had to have a purpose, she would have figured that sure enough. Too smart not to. But even if her figuring had got real cute and she had walked round the problem till the answers were staring her in the face, what could she do, who could she tell?

Nobody. Not a soul from here to Eldron, save them wandering Apache, and if she happened across them, talking Winchesters would be the last thing on their minds! No, whichever way you viewed it, she was on her own, just a burr loose in the boot. Answer to that, of course, was to take off the boot and shake the burr free.

He would too, he decided, tonight at the Claw when the woman came crawling in. Shake her free of him for good, but not before. . . .

He grinned and pushed at the floppy hat. He would leave what was left of her for the Apache. Keep them happy and off his butt. Least he could do.

Ratrap patted the Bible box and went back to watching the shadows. The enemy were closing in.

Goose Farrars was hungry, thirsty, dust-drenched and irritable. This day had not been one of the best. The drifters had been a troublesome diversion he could have well done without, fond as he was of cleaning through his Colt with meaningful lead. Ratrap was fidgeting over that woman; the boys were worn and impatient and the girls were getting frisky for some town life. Wagons were no substitute for beds, they reckoned, no matter who was sharing them. The sooner they reached the Claw the better, and the sooner they hit Eldron the better still.

And then there was that high shadow drifting the peaks. Been there on and off for more than an hour; just drifting, sometimes hidden behind crags, sometimes lost in boulders, but always back again, always there, keeping pace, like it was watching.

So was it? Was the shadow one of those marauding Apache, the scout-eyes measuring the wagons' pace, checking on their route? Maybe. It would figure if the Apache had empty stomachs and a yearning for women, but they were leaving it awful late for an attack. Should have made their move long before now. No Apache, however hungry, would risk a break out at dusk.

So maybe it was somebody else, and there was only one man fool enough, desperate enough, to trail the Drift in that fashion – Marshal Sam Cavendish. He would chance it for another grab at Ratrap, play his hand till the fingers were numb for an opportunity to see Moses stretching rope. Hell, he had been trying for close on a whole year!

But maybe not quite like this, especially now that he seemed to have drifted on, as if getting ahead of them. Nothing to be gained by that, not one man trailing loose, no matter how fast his gun.

No, Marshal Cavendish was going to have to wait till the outfits cleared the Drift and headed for town, and by then it would be far too late. It would all be over, blood-soaked and lead-splintered before the lawman could blink let alone draw. And maybe he would be right in the firing line!

So no point in saying anything to Ratrap. Best leave him to his obsession with that spooky widow and hope she turned up again, and this time for the last time. She was going nowhere from here on, rest on it.

Goose Farrars rubbed his aching stomach and spat Drift dirt. Just one hell of a day!

The Claw was a freak of nature. It should never have been there, never have existed or been thought even possible in a place like the Drinkwater Drift.

But it was and had been for as long as anybody could remember, and no man crossing that eerie, arid land could ever forget it. Miss the Claw, trail clear of it, fail to find it, and you had not only passed up the only watering-hole in a hundred miles of parched dirt and rock, but put your marker on a death warrant. There was nothing after the Claw should you trail by it save the certainty of a slow, painful demise to crow meat. There were bones enough to prove it on the final push to the promised lands beyond.

Moses Ratrap had no such doubts of his where-abouts that early evening as he turned his wagons from the main trail to the clutch of high rocks where the Claw's deep, limpid pool of cool water lay like a gem on a carpet of rags.

And relieved to the very last strand of his guts he surely was to see it, he thought, smiling broadly to himself at his first glimpse of the softly shadowed haven. No man, he figured, could ask for more at a time like this, and some long gone to dust now would have given a fortune for the chance.

63

But Ratrap had been this way before – yessir, he knew his Drinkwater well enough, which was why, of course, he had chosen to trail it *en route* to his mission at Eldron. Know your Drift, he had reasoned, and you had the key to the door few could find let alone open.

He was pleased, satisfied, almost content as he shouted his orders for the wagons to circle at the pool.

'Secure tight for the night, boys and gals, and yuh got y'selves a heaven 'til sun-up!' he had yelled as the first of the girls were stripping to plunge to the water's welcome.

Maybe he would open up that cask of whiskey he had back of his wagon, he was thinking, as he slid from his outfit, yawned and stretched; cook up a meal, get to that cask and the girls, and come tomorrow ... well, maybe just three days to Eldron, time to ready up for the job in hand and then, when it was all done, head deeper West taking with him whatever he fancied.

A fine wholesome prospect, he thought. And so it should be. Hell, the whole thing had been more than twelve months in the planning!

Detail, that was the measure of it all; attention to detail and the closer look to be sure you had it right. Never get taken by surprise, not if you wanted. . . .

It had been then, as Moses Ratrap scanned the rims of the rocks and boulders surrounding the

pool, that same self-satisfied smirk across his
face, his eyes gleaming, that he had pushed
angrily at the brim of his floppy hat, blinked and
growled deep in his throat.

Damn it, that woman was there – right there,
straddling a boulder above the pool like she was
some goddamn nymph; smiling, waving, still
wrapped in that shred of a dress, but as mock-
ingly fresh to the trail-ragged traveller as a
cactus flower.

And, hell, now that was a surprise!

Nine

'Let me take her out now, Moses. One shot, that's all it'll be. Clean and sure. One shot.' Goose Farrars fingered the Winchester cradled in his arms as if soothing a new-born, his gaze narrowed to dark slits on the woman seated at ease on the boulder. 'We don't do it now,' he croaked, 'we'll live to rue the day. I'm tellin' yuh, friend. Hear me.'

'I hear yuh, Goose, I do indeed,' said Ratrap without the faintest blink across his eyes, his voice soft, words gentle, a slow smile twitching over his lips. 'But I ain't so sure. No, I ain't so sure. . . .'

'Don't wait, f'Crissake,' croaked Goose again. 'She ain't worth it. Nothin' like.' His grip tightened on the rifle. 'Been a bad omen since we happened across her. Written on her face. Yuh can see it. Bitch!'

'Yeah,' murmured Ratrap, still staring, still unblinking. 'Yeah, yuh can at that, can't yuh?

66

Some woman, eh, some woman. We ain't crossed a woman like that before. Not no how, no way.'

Goose spat quietly into the dirt, glanced quickly at the others grouped in silence round the watering-hole. Damn it, he thought, spitting again, anybody would think they were seeing a ghost, a body back from the dead. 'Hell, Moses,' he hissed, 'don't get to procrastinatin' now. This ain't the time. Look at the others, will yuh? They're waitin' on yuh word. All yuh gotta do is say it, f'Crissake! What yuh waitin' for?'

'I ain't waitin', Goose, I'm admirin'.'

'*Admirin*'? What the hell's there to admire?' groaned Goose. 'She ain't no paintin', damn it. That woman's sure as Drift dirt a pain in the butt, and she ain't gettin' no easier. I'm tellin' yuh, Moses, tellin' yuh straight—'

'But not truly thinkin', are yuh, Goose? Not loosin' it round in that baked brain of yours just what that woman up there really means.'

'I know damn well what she means, sure enough,' snapped Goose. 'She means trouble. Big trouble. Big as it comes.'

'Bein' there,' said Ratrap calmly, his slow smile twitching faster, 'just sittin' there ain't no accident, is it now? T'ain't no miracle of survival for the woman to be here ahead of us lookin' like she's had a whole afternoon to freshen up. Nossir. Good Lord may have His ways, my friend, but even He don't get to foolin' the Drinkwater that easy.'

67

'Don't get to makin' a deal of difference, does it?' drawled Goose, shifting the Winchester impatiently. 'She's here – how she did it ain't worth a breath of cuss. Gettin' rid of her, permanent as it ever gets, is what counts, and I'm all for doin' it right this minute.' He raised the rifle to his shoulder. 'Like I say, just one clean shot, straight through that pretty head of hers. . . .'

'Hmm,' murmured Ratrap, flicking at the brim of his hat, 'but then we ain't never goin' to know whose hand guided her here, are we?'

Hell, that was a hair's-breadth close, sighed Cavendish, swallowing dirt over his chilled throat. Another spit of a second. . . . But why had Farrars hesitated? Why was he lowering the rifle and staring at Ratrap as if clapping eyes on some devil? What had he said that had curbed the shot? Hell!

The marshal eased his position high in the rocks above the watering-hole and narrowed his focus tight against the fast fading light. Another half-hour and there would be nothing to see save the dark shapes flitting through Ratrap's campfires.

But the woman had made it – damn it, she had! – and calm as a basking rattler was baiting the old Bible-puncher like some classy whore. Maybe, but was Ratrap taken in by it? He was a weathered, long-time dealer at the sharper end of life and no easy edge to blunt. Goose had seemed to be all for finishing Ellie Gates then and there but had been halted by Moses. And that, thought Cavendish, threw a whole heap of questions into the pot.

Was Ratrap saving the woman for his personal pleasure, or had he already sniffed out some cunning in her being at the Claw ahead of him? And just what had he said to Goose that had persuaded the trigger-itchy sidekick to lower his rifle and stare like he had? Farrars' thinking was shoot first and ponder later.

'Hell,' hissed Cavendish again, blinking against the gloom, that woman was playing a game she could lose as easy as flicking a pebble to that pool of clear water – and he had let her do it, gone along with the whole crazy scheme, was here right now watching it begin to whatever its miserable end.

He should have talked her out of it. Damn it, dragged her kicking and screaming out of the Drift if need be! But he wanted Ratrap, that more than anything, and Ellie Gates wanted. . . . A strange peace of mind in revenge, or had the events since Duncan so warped her thinking she no longer cared, much less considered? If she was going to die. . . .

He swallowed. It was done. It was happening, and now the only priority was to stay in touch, out of sight, keep those late-night rendezvous for the woman's messages, and just hope.

Full dark was close but not that close, moving in fast, but not this fast, not crashing in across the back of his skull in a searing, blinding flash, not dropping like a curtain so that he was suddenly sightless, his thoughts spinning to oblivion. No, this was not nightfall.

Sam Cavendish had only half-turned to face the man at his back, caught no more than a blurred glimpse of the raised arm, the rock clutched in claw-tight fingers, but had seen just enough of the attacker's eyes to recognize the gleam of Apache stealth.

And then he saw nothing, not even the night.

Moses Ratrap stared at the woman with the look of a man who could not yet decide if what he was about to sample would prove a fine liquor or the first dose of carefully disguised poison.

But he was in no hurry to find out. He could wait. This night was still young and had some way to go.

'Well, now,' he grinned, shifting his weight from one foot to the other, his gaze tight and narrowed on Ellie Gates where she leaned, arms folded across her, on the wagon wheel, 'ain't you just somethin', ma'am. Real somethin'. Not many come this far state you were in; so tell me – how'd yuh do it, eh? Yuh got some stamina I ain't never heard tell of before?'

'Survival, mister,' said Ellie through a half smile that hid the chill of fear at her back. 'Plain survival. Yuh'd know about that, wouldn't yuh?'

'Oh, sure, ma'am, sure, been at it all my life. Know the feelin'. But if yuh so good at it, how come yuh didn't just keep on goin', eh? How come yuh joined up here again? No guarantee I'd welcome yuh after high-tailin' it like yuh did. Nothin' to say I am, is there? Could just as easy—'

'But you won't,' said Ellie firmly, with a slight toss of her hair as her arms unfolded and spread along the wagon. 'No, I'm bankin' on yuh takin' me outa this place to wherever yuh goin'. Can't manage that all by m'self. So. . . .' She let the smile grow slowly. 'There'll be a price, o'course, but I'll pay – whatever the currency.'

Ellie felt a soft trickle of sweat in her neck, dampening the palms of her hands, as Ratrap's gaze widened and he licked anxiously at his lips.

Had she done enough, she wondered, laid as much of the right bait as would tempt? Would Ratrap grab now while his followers wallowed like cattle at the pool? But would that be too soon? She had to know more, a whole lot more, before—

'Moses? We got trouble!'

The voice of Goose Farrars cracked across the darkness like a gunshot. There was a sudden, tensed silence at the pool, a stillness broken only

71

by the scuffing of boots through dirt, the dragging of a limp, heavy weight, and then the sight of Farrars dumping a dead, blood-soaked body at Ratrap's feet.

'Charlie Benns,' croaked Goose. 'One of the look-outs. Throat cut.' He spat viciously. 'Apache's doin'.'

Ratrap stepped to the body, stared at it then at Goose. 'That close?' he murmured.

'Too damn close!' snarled Goose. 'Mebbe no more than a handful, scavengin' party out for what they can get, but they could sure as hell hold us up. Might mean we're a day late at Eldron, and we can't afford to miss—'

'I'll do the figurin'!' snapped Ratrap. 'You just make sure we're ready to pull out first touch of light.'

'Told yuh that woman'd mean trouble,' muttered Goose. 'Said as how—'

Ratrap kicked at the dirt. 'Don't figure!' he bellowed. 'Don't none of yuh figure! I do the figurin' round here for everybody. Got it?' He turned to glare at Ellie. 'You 'specially,' he croaked.

Ellie shivered in the suddenly chill night air and pulled her flat, bewildered gaze from the body of Charlie Benns. The fear began to grip again, dry her throat to grit, trickle the sweat to ice. There had never been a burned-out wagon back there on the trail, and that scalp had been a long

72

past trophy, but, hell, there had been Apaches!

She shivered again and gazed wide-eyed into the mask of night hills. Where are you now, Sam Cavendish, she wondered?

Just where are you now?

Ten

It was long into that night before Marshal Sam Cavendish had the remotest notion of where he was or how he had ever come to be there, and then only thanks to the sudden splash of water in his face, the kick buried deep in his ribs, a hand gripping his hair and threatening to uproot most of it, and the snarled grunt into his face.

He was thrown back against the rock, watched for a moment by the grinning, moon-eyed Apache, kicked again and finally left to gather whatever senses he could summon.

Few and far between, it seemed: a throbbing, hammer-heavy pain in his head, sore ribs, aching muscles, hands unmoving in the tight binding of rope, eyes fiery with blurred vision, and a throat hardly worth the effort of swallowing on.

Nothing like a promising outlook, he reckoned, staying motionless against the rock, but alive and still breathing, for now.

But for how long?

It was another long ten minutes before he could trust to anything coming into focus through the darkness. Apaches for certain, six, maybe eight of them gathered in a huddle in the cover of thick boulders. Planning what to do with him, or plotting their next move at first light? Both, he reckoned.

Doubtless he was being saved for some later 'entertainment'. And not much doubt either what they planned come the first hint of sunlight – an attack on Ratrap's wagons, more than likely while they were still drawn up at the Claw. But no screaming, headlong rush out of the hills. No, these marauders would have sized up Ratrap's numbers and strength and be planning the tactics to suit.

Maybe they would let the wagons pull out and then follow like scavenging termites, eating slowly into the outfits until they were no more than bones rattling through the Drift. Or maybe they would pin them down at the Claw, wait for the madness to set in. Either way, Ratrap would have to come up with some smart answers.

And he just might at that. But the hell with Ratrap. What about Ellie Gates?

It had been the thought of the woman's fate that had jolted Cavendish back to sharp reality. She had shown she had guts, courage too, even though both might be sparked by some crazy obsession, but handling Ratrap for what she had

75

in mind was one thing; taking on the Bible-puncher *and* a bunch of mean-minded Apaches something else. Just how did she figure. . . .

Cavendish groaned deep in his pinched throat and closed his eyes. Ellie Gates would have to look to herself right now. Priority for him was clear enough, but how to tackle it he had not the slightest notion.

He licked at a line of cold sweat at his lips, blinked his eyes open again and wondered how long to sun-up – or maybe more to the point, how long to live?

Ellie Gates eased away from the glow of the night fire and the resentful gazes of the girls gathered round it and sought the deeper darkness. Last thing she was looking for at this time was any hint of a confrontation with the family. Whole situation was tinder-dry as it was. It only needed a word, a glance, to fan new flames, and with Ratrap and Goose Farrars in their present mood that might lead to almost anything.

Another dead body, very definitely hers, was only one option.

She slid deeper through the night towards the wagon she and Joe had trailed out of Duncan. There was a box of papers, inks, pens somewhere in there, just one of the seemingly useless items grabbed in the frenzy on that night of flight.

Writing materials, when another dress would have been. . . . What the hell, pen and paper might be a life-line through the next few days if they were the means to the messages she could leave on the trail for Cavendish.

She slid towards the deserted wagon. Only good thing about the threat of Apaches was the disposal of Ratrap's men to look-out posts. Not a sign right now of any one of them guarding her wagon. Two minutes were all she would need, just long enough to get to the pine box where she had always kept the pens, another minute to write the message – *Destination Eldron* – and be all through in four at most. She would fathom how and where to leave the paper later. The rest would be up to Cavendish.

She was at the wagon now, tense and stiff, listening for sounds, her eyes flicking anxiously for movement. All quiet, she decided, and nobody close. She moved quickly to the rear flap, pulled it aside and peered inside.

Hell, the wagon was empty! Not a stick, not a remnant, nothing. Only space.

'Cleared it out day yuh made the run,' came the drawled, mocking words at her back. 'Not a deal of much worth holdin' to.'

Ellie turned sharply to face the grinning glare of Goose Farrars, her eyes wide with the rush of panic, her fear tingling at her spine.

'Didn't figure yuh for bein' back,' said Farrars,

77

slouching to one side ' 'Course, if there's somethin' special yuh want—'

'No, nothin',' clipped Ellie, forcing a smile. 'I was just wonderin'—'

'Ain't the time for wonderin', lady. Not right now. Them Apache out there'll be gettin' fidgety come another hour, kinda anxious to get a samplin' of the main cargo we're carryin'. Yuh follow, ma'am?' Farrars asked coldly. 'I'm talkin' about your kind, women kind, 'specially white. Apache delicacy, or mebbe yuh knew that already, eh? Figured it for y'self, seein' as how yuh seem to do a whole lot of that.'

'I'm aware of what yuh sayin', mister,' said Ellie, stiffening.

'Good, 'cus it might just come to yuh gettin' a closer look if Ratrap gets to doin' some tradin'.'

'Tradin'?' frowned Ellie. 'What yuh mean?'

'Coupla women would guarantee a safe passage outa here,' drawled Farrars. 'We could spare that, 'specially if you happened to be one of 'em.'

'You'd hand over women to Apaches?' murmured Ellie. 'You'd do a thing like that?'

'Ratrap would. I know him. Ain't nothin' goin' to stop him hittin' Eldron right on time. Not nothin'.'

Ellie stiffened again, her eyes narrowing. 'And what's so special about Eldron yuh'd trade women for?'

Farrars' eyes gleamed as his grin broke to a wide smile. 'Gold – as much of it as a man could

78

ever handle. Enough gold to—'

'Goose, get y'self here,' called Ratrap from the fire. 'I got an idea.'

'You bet he has!' said Farrars cynically. 'You bet on it! I'd stay outa sight if I were you, lady, deep as yuh can go while it's still dark. Ain't goin' to be much to look to once that sun clears them hills.'

Ellie shivered as Farrars walked away to the fire glow. Time to run again, she wondered, get back to Cavendish? She knew enough now for the marshal to make his move. There was nothing to stay here for, no need for pens and paper. She had got what she had come for faster than she could ever have hoped. Now was the time to cut again – this time for good.

'Not so fast, ma'am,' snapped Ratrap, closing on her as if from nowhere. 'Seein' as how yuh so kindly came back to us, might as well get yuh to helpin' out in this hour of need, eh? Yuh agree? Share and share alike. One for all and all for one. Why, sure yuh do. Got somethin' real special in mind for yuh. Real special.'

Eleven

Thirty minutes – and every one of them a nugget
of gold as far as Sam Cavendish was concerned.
He squinted anxiously into the sprawling aura of
grey breaking across the eastern skies, then,
conscious of a nerve twitching in his cheek, at the
group of Apaches.

They had stayed quiet through the night hours,
their concentration on the surrounding cover of
rocks, tensed it seemed for the slightest sound,
almost unaware of Cavendish and glancing only
occasionally in his direction. They were content
enough for now to simply hold him, but for what,
he wondered? Some kind of hostage to be bartered
later? Maybe, but where and what or who would
be the asking price? Might be days away. Apaches
had a patience that was timeless.

Cavendish, on the other hand, had neither time
at his disposal nor the patience to contemplate it.
He had just those thirty minutes before the first
light blinked and the Apaches made their move.

They would hit the wagons while the shadows were still blurred in the early dawn, when Ratrap and his followers would be at their most vulnerable: sleep weary, nervy, uncertain and far from keen enough at that hour to spot subtle Apache stalking. They would close silently, drifting like a touch of breath through the rocks, in no hurry, watching every movement, aware of every shift of dirt.

They were outnumbered and knew it. Ratrap could muster twice as many guns against the seven Apache who would make the strike, one man being left in the rocks to guard the ponies and Cavendish. But sheer numbers had never been a burr in the boot to attack-happy, hungry Apache, not when the real prize in Ratrap's wagons was white women – Ellie Gates among them.

Cavendish grunted softly against his tumbling thoughts and went back to working the rope binding his wrists behind him across the jagged edge of rock. Slow, rough going that was maybe as pointless as it was desperate, but was there anything else? Only chance he had, he figured, remote as it was, lay in freeing himself by the time he was alone with the single look-out Apache. Given that frail break, he might, just might. . . .

He flinched as a single strand parted. That was the first. Hell, how long to go before the rope had weakened enough to part? Another hour, two?

Damn it, he had thirty minutes!

He stiffened at the sudden bout of excited murmuring among the Indians. They were readying up, turning now to face the lifting light, waiting a moment for the leader among them to take a last look round, glance at Cavendish but make no move to cross to him. He muttered a set of instructions to the younger buck who would guard the ponies, patted him on the shoulder and led the others into the shadowed rocks.

Now what? Would the guard check on his prisoner, make sure that rope was tight knotted? Not yet. He was more concerned with the ponies, loose-hitched but anxious to be moving. Take your time, fellow, thought Cavendish, leave whatever there is to me!

Another strand parted, easier this time. He could feel a loosening now. Might not take more than. . . . The guard had turned, was staring at him as if some sixth sense had sounded a warning. Cavendish half-closed his eyes, hung his head despondently, twitched in a mock doze, watched the Apache make as if to step towards him, then relax again and turn back to the ponies.

Fellow was edgy. Maybe this was his first raid, blooding himself to the ways of the renegade hunting party, tensed at the thoughts of what was to come, conscious of the trust placed in him, but maybe a mite disappointed at being overlooked for the real action.

He would learn fast, thought Cavendish, but not fast enough if he stayed where he was!

A third strand parted. The marshal flexed his fingers, twisted his wrists through the remaining strands. One more, just one, and he would risk the tug. He glanced at the sky. Almost full light now. Ratrap would be geared for the attack, Winchesters trained like eyes on metal stalks on the surrounding hills. Might make a run for it once he realized the Apaches were on foot. Might be his best chance, give him a few miles start. Or would he sit it out? Maybe that depended on. . . .

The fourth strand snapped clear. Cavendish relaxed, opened his eyes wide on the guard's back. Stay right there, he thought, tensing for the tug to free his arms. He began to sweat, warm, sticky sweat that bubbled on the skin and bit like flies. His head throbbed, a vein pulsed at his temple, his vision swam, blurred, came back into focus, tight and concentrated.

And then he moved!

He was free and scrambling to his feet before the young Apache's senses could react. No silent, subtle approach now. Priority was simple enough: get to the buck and take him out before the ponies were spooked into pulling clear of the line.

Not so easy.

The Apache had turned seconds before Cavendish's hands could make the grab at his shoulders. He crouched for an instant, eyes

83

gleaming, then sidestepped the marshal with the speed and agility of a startled rat and brought a leg round in a swinging arc to bury the foot deep in the marshal's gut.

Cavendish gasped, groaned, stumbled forward, arms flaying on the air like blown branches. He crashed to the dirt only feet from the already shuffling ponies, half-turned but had the Apache straddling him before he could blink the dust clear.

He saw the flash of a blade, raised a hand for a grip on the Apache's wrist, settled his fingers on a forearm and gritted his teeth in the effort to heave the knife out of reach of his throat.

The Apache hissed and grunted, held his breath against the summoning of greater strength for the downward plunge of the blade, grinned as he felt the marshal's resistance weakening under a lathering of sweat.

Damn it, the buck had the edge, thought Cavendish, the strength of youth, the will to draw blood. Now the blade was within a whisker of flesh, almost brushing the marshal's throat. He could sense the chill of it and might be no more than a breath away from its final searing thrust.

Cavendish tightened his grip, pushed, tried to roll clear and knew then that he was pinned there like some lame prey at the teeth of hunger. Hell, if only there was one more ounce of strength. . . .

He saw the rush of the pony's hoof in a panic-stricken kick as if watching an avalanche of shadows, heard the crack as it crashed across the Apache's skull, then the dazed, bewildered look on the buck's face, the swirling eyes, heard the anguished cry that bubbled in the man's open mouth, and was scrambling free of the suddenly limp body before it sprawled, lifeless and drained, in the dirt.

He choked, spat, shook his head, fought the tremble through his limbs and rolled again as the ponies snorted, pranced and heaved against the hitch-line.

It was a full half-minute then before Cavendish had regained his senses and was seeing clear-eyed and straight again.

He struggled to his feet, sweat-soaked, his mind reeling, and staggered to the hitch-line. The ponies were already lathered to a frenzy, kicking, bucking, snorting, straining to be free and running. He gathered the halter lines and took the strain of the tossing heads, murmuring softly as he eased closer. How long, he wondered, before the Apaches in the rocks became suspicious enough of the noise to investigate? Were they already alerted? Or were they too preoccupied with the wagons now to care?

Cavendish stood his ground as the ponies calmed and began to settle, his thoughts racing to his next move.

Scatter the ponies and make for the Claw? But

to do what? He had no weapon, save for the Apache's knife. Where was his own mount? The mare, fully saddled with his Winchester safe in its scabbard, had been back of the rocks when the Apaches had taken him. So had she bolted, or was she still wandering close by? Maybe he should make, for that same spot, track the mount down, but had he the time, would he cross the Apaches' tracks again – he was in no shape for another hand-to-hand fight – and what of Ratrap and the wagons?

What, damn it, of Ellie Gates?

The silence and stillness came suddenly. The ponies relaxed, Cavendish breathed easy. He waited, listening, watching the light spread like a long grey stain over the night sky, stepped carefully round the body of the Apache guard, collected the buck's knife, and slid away to the cover of the rocks.

Leave the ponies hitched, he had decided, let the Apaches at the Claw think all was as it should be; give himself the time now to get closer to the wagons, seek out the mare if she had not already strayed deep into the Drift, and then. . . .

It was the sudden chill across the sweat in Cavendish's neck that halted him and forced him to crouch instinctively among the shadows. A breeze, as unexpected as snowfall, stiff and keen, swinging in from the east with the dawn light. But no ordinary breeze, he thought, lifting his gaze to the sudden scudding of bruised, broken cloud. This was a breeze you could hear as well as feel; a whistling, whining breeze that gathered on itself like a wheezing breath before the violent cough.

He came upright again, narrowed his eyes against the stinging edge of the blow and stared east. 'Hell,' he rasped, 'that's all I need!' and licked at the first gritty swirl of dirt at his lips.

Sandstorm!

Twelve

The breeze broke free to a frenzied wind within seconds. First light was smothered in a shroud of drifting grey dirt and swirling sand. Where once there had been silence and calm there was now a morning filled with a haunting whine and distant roar that ripped through Cavendish's head until he thought it would either take off or crack where it fought to stay steady on his neck and shoulders.

It had taken some minutes for him to decide to move into a tighter grip of rocks. No point now in looking to the ponies – they would simply turn their backs on the storm and stand firm till it passed – and no chance either of making it to the Claw. Only consolation there was that the Apaches would be similarly pinned down and forced to wait.

But would Ratrap?

Hell, he was just about crazed enough to make a dash for it under the storm's cover, claim the onset as some Divine intervention and Heaven-sent. And he could be right at that! Fellow had only to step five yards and he would be out of sight, not so much as a blur or sound against the raging wind and twisting rush of flying sand. If the old Bible-puncher could keep his teams moving he would be lost in an hour. Stay where he was and he would be buried. Easy pickings when the Apaches stirred again.

Ratrap would risk the dash, no question, and scatter the losses to the Devil.

Cavendish spat more dirt as he strained and struggled through the rocks, his eyes narrowed to the tightest slits, hands reaching ahead of him as if to shove the dirt aside, breath rasping with the effort. He staggered a yard, slid back two, battled again until he was bent double, buffeted from side to side, swept at random with all the ease of some loose, uprooted straggle of brush.

He cursed, fell to his knees, gave himself up for a moment to the onslaught and crawled to the nearest rock. Nothing else for it, he reckoned, this was as far as it went. He was going nowhere, not till the storm eased and he could open his eyes to see more than a hand ahead of him.

He curled to a ball behind the rock, ground his teeth over grit and relaxed. All he needed to do was stay breathing.

Meantime, the sand could have him. And it would, damn it!

'Storm rage! Tempest devour! Lordy, hallelujah, ain't this just the day for it! Lordy, Lordy! Hallelujah!'

Moses Ratrap's voice crashed against the howl of the wind and was blown aside to an echoing whine as he leaned against the blast, his hands white with dust on the reins, face a grey mask pitted with eyes and gaping mouth, the rags of his clothing swirling about him like vast, storm-lashed sails. The team snorted and whinnied in their heaving, slithering effort to haul the wagon, shuddered as Goose Farrars drew his outfit along-side, but plunged on in a creaking, groaning splutter of timbers and grinding wheels.

'We ain't never goin' to make it,' yelled Goose, rolling to the pitch of the wind, his eyes near blinded by sand and dirt. 'Horses ain't up to it. Me neither! Best hole up till this is blown through.'

'No way, no way, my friend!' called Ratrap, spitting sand, then grinning like some fevered phantom. 'This is the Good Lord's doin', His way. Don't yuh feel it, Goose? Ain't the Good Word coursin' through yuh blood, holdin' to yuh bones?'

'All I got coursin' through me is godforsaken Drift dirt and a sonofabitch wind!'

'That's 'cus yuh ain't given to the faith, my son, yuh ain't lettin' it guide and be the spirit of yuh bein'.'

90

'Hang it, Moses,' bellowed Goose almost blown clear of his outfit in a thrusting gust, last thing on my mind right now is spirit, savin' what I should be drinkin' if I had so much as a two-bit ounce of sense! I'm tellin' yuh, good and loud, straight up, we ain't—'

'I hear yuh, Mr Farrars, I hear yuh, but I ain't listenin' to no fool backin'-down talk. We're goin' on, yuh hear *that*, mister, straight on, into the eye of this 'ere storm and out the other side, clear of this goddamn Drift and down the trail to Eldron. And there ain't nothin', nothin' breathin', livin' on this God's earth, goin' to stop us.' He screamed at the horses. 'Yuh hearin' all this, Goose? I sure as hell hope yuh are, 'cus I ain't spellin' it out no more and I ain't wastin' effort on the sayin'. Now, yuh fix that woman good and safe back there?'

'Sure, I did,' yelled Goose, his words hollow on the searing wind. 'Just like yuh said, strapped tight to her wagon. Them Apache bucks'll see her soon as the storm's passed.'

'Smell her long before that!' grinned Ratrap. 'They won't be followin', not once they get their sweaty hands on her, they won't. Pity. Would've preferred that pleasure for m'self. No worry – there'll be more, plenty more, any amount once we're all through at Eldron. And Eldron, mister, is all we're here for. Coupla days and then all the livin' yuh want! Meantime, yuh get a hold of that outfit, my son, and yuh keep the family safe, eh?'

Ratrap leaned into the wind again and cracked the reins to the howling gusts. 'Hallelujah! The Lord giveth, Mr Farrars, and He sure ain't takin' nothin' away, not this day He ain't!'

'Wouldn't set too much on His mood t'morrow, though!' groaned Goose to nothing and no one save the grey swirl of the storm.

Ellie Gates had reckoned herself for dead an hour ago. She should have been no more than sun and sand-scorched skin and bone by now, a mound of torn rags closely resembling something that had once been a woman just into her thirtieth year. There should have been nothing of her worth the bother of a second glance, save what could be bundled into some shallow grave. No cause either for a marker. Suffice it that somebody trailing the Drinkwater Drift had come across her roped to the wheel of a broken-down wagon and done the decent thing. How she had got there was no business of the passing stranger.

But she was not dead and nothing like it.

She was maybe wishing for an end to close in, but with every gasp, every lungful of the hot, dirt-drenched air, she was surviving, clinging instinctively to life, however worthless, empty and burned through.

And with every cough and spit into that sand and wind swirling morning of storm, she was spitting into the leering face of Moses Ratrap, defying

him to the last, dragging him to whatever hell
awaited.

Not so far away, she thought, her eyes closing
against the driving grit. Storm would blow itself
out long before noon, and with the calm, the
sudden bursts of sunlight scattering the grey dust
light, would come the marauding Apaches. There
would be no half measures then; simply the
taking of her until they were all through and she
was clean out of her mind. Maybe then they would
move on, trail Ratrap's wagons for whatever other
pickings might come to hand.

She shuddered against another howling blast
of wind, struggled uselessly against the ropes
binding her to the wheel, and pondered once
again on the fate of Marshal Sam Cavendish.

But did she need to? If there was anything
more certain than the fate awaiting her, it was the
hell that had sure as day caught up with
Cavendish. He must have fallen to the Apaches at
nightfall, she reckoned, stood nothing of a chance
and been smothered to silence in minutes.

So much for his long pursuit of Ratrap; so much
for coming within a whisker of reaching him. As
with so many who had risked the Drift as a last
resort, the final fingertip on some distant hope,
the Drift had won. Only the likes of Moses Ratrap
went on – a godforsaken land at one with its kind
in a godforsaken man!

Hell, she cursed through a rasping gasp, spitting sand, and once into Eldron the sonofabitch and his family and their mint condition Winchesters would take a haul of gold.

Whose gold, from where, to where, and why Eldron?

Who cared? It hardly mattered right now. All that really stood to take account of was the wind, the sand, the dead grey light, and the noon-day calm that would be here soon enough.

Maybe by then she would be truly dead, as stiff and lifeless as the stranger Joe had shot in the street at Duncan, whose shadow had pushed them to the Drift. To no avail.

That same shadow was still closing in.

Thirteen

Cavendish flexed a finger, an arm, an elbow, then a leg, and could almost hear the piled sand grind away, grain by shifting grain.

He blinked, spat dirt and dared himself to widen his gaze over the first hint of changing light. The wind had eased back now to a slow, murmuring roll gathered among the higher ranges, the sand settled to scurrying waves over firmer ground. Somewhere, far above him on a distant crag, a hawk flapped into grateful life, screeched and swooped to the faintest shimmer of sunlight.

Cavendish spat again, came achingly from a ball to his knees, ran a hand over his face and wondered if there was any place across his body not invaded by sand. He knuckled his eyes into focus and steadied his gaze. The dirt had been driven by the wind to a sea of sculpted waves, piled itself in twisted shapes against the flatter surfaces of rock, and here and there been driven high to sprawl like hunchback lizards on the boulder heads. There were no sounds now, no movements.

So where were the Apaches; had Ratrap made the dash; what had happened to Ellie Gates?

It took only seconds then for the marshal to find his feet, take in his bearings and trudge away through the ankle-deep sand towards the rim of the Claw.

He hugged the half shadows of darkness wherever they could be reached, but held to a steady, thrusting pace. No point now in trying to scout out Apaches. If they were there and close enough they had seen him and had him in their sights. Damn all he could do if they decided to shoot. Getting where he wanted to be would be all down to luck, and that had been in short supply of late! Who was to say it would change?

He had come to within only yards of where he had left the mare and climbed to his vantage point overlooking the Claw, when he halted, sniffed and closed on the nearest shadow.

He knew that smell well enough – hell, he should, it had been as much a part of his life these past years as his boots. The mare! She had been here, maybe sheltering against the storm, and not long back, but how far had she strayed once the blow had passed? Or had those Apaches. . . ? The smell drifted to him again, this time closer, fresher.

Oh, yes, he thought, she was close, almost to hand. *But was she alone?* If the Apache had got to her they would have the mount loose-roped as bait to lure him. Only one way to decide that, he figured, and slapped his hand twice across his thigh. No need to do more.

The mare was there, right there – and almost before he had realized, rounding the boulders clearing the cleft, trotting towards him, tail swishing, head frisking, fully saddled, the Winchester tight in its scabbard.

Fine, just fine, thought Cavendish. But what, in that case, was keeping the Apaches so occupied?

A whispered word to the mare, a reassuring pat, and seconds later Cavendish was trailing through the driven sand on a line that would bring him to the foot of the Claw and the watering-hole.

He went silently, the mare's steps softened on the dirt drifts, and with no more thought for the surrounding rocks and crags than he had for the clearing sky and strengthening sunlight. He had only one thought, and it was growing darker by the minute; images that licked like flame and were fanned by an anger that was already raising sweat in his neck and back even as he broached the rim of a slope that ran clear to the flat, placid water and gave an unbroken view of the Drift trail beyond.

Cavendish licked his lips anxiously as he

reined to a halt. His eyes narrowed, aching and sand sore, and his hand reached instinctively for the rifle butt.

No time then for watching, for debating what might or might not be done, for the hesitation in a second thought or the sharper realization that the Apaches out there had an edge of nearly two to one. No seconds when he might have wondered how many he would take out before he fell; only the resolve that in the volley of returned fire he would make certain he had one shot for his last target.

Ellie Gates was never going to see the sun come full up on the Drinkwater Drift, not this day, not if he failed her.

And then Cavendish gave the mare her head.

She responded at the first slackening of rein, slipping away to the uncertain surface of sand as if raised to it, aware of only one destination, conscious of her rider already leaning low to her neck.

The marshal's gaze was steady now on the shimmering scene ahead of him: the wagon, one side of it jutting like a black thigh bone from the covering of sand; the Apaches, seven of them, five dragging the limp, half-naked body of Ellie Gates across the dirt to the nearest rocks, two ransacking the outfit for whatever had been left; the shadows in the half light dancing round them like giant fingers, and not a sound, not a whimper, cry

or breath to be heard, as if the whole were being
played out through a silent dream.

Ratrap – this was Moses Ratrap's doing,
thought Cavendish, sensing the mare gain level
ground, only he would have a mind infested bad
enough to leave a woman. . . . 'Damn the sonofabitch to Hell!' he yelled as he brought the
Winchester to his shoulder and released the
vicious lead.

The Apaches still at the wagon were thrown
back instantly. Cavendish veered the mare to the
right as the bucks abandoned their prize and slid
to their bellies like lizards, rifles probing from the
sand in a swinging arc levelled and firing wildly
almost before Cavendish had time to sling himself
lower.

The mare snorted, stretched to a faster gallop,
tossed her head as Cavendish nudged his weight
to her flank to indicate an attack head-on. Again,
she responded without effort, steadying the pace
precisely to the marshal's next burst of firing. He
heard a yell, a scream, nudged for more speed and
saw the bodies of the bucks through a blur of
swirling sand and dirt and flying sweat.

But were they dead or still alive? How many
had he hit? How many were merely winged? How
long, damn it, before *they* got lucky?

The mare raced on, faster, smoother, until it
seemed her every muscle was pulsing to the
excitement of momentum and the smell of blood.

'At 'em, gal, at 'em!' croaked Cavendish through a sand-lined mouth, a dirt-stiff throat, struggling now to bring the Winchester level and into aim.

His finger was tensed on the trigger, his arm rigid for the steady firing, eyes wide and blood-shot against the rush of air, when the mare faltered, a foreleg hoof clipping a buried rock.

She stumbled, snorted, whinnied high and shrill and crashed to her left, throwing Cavendish clear in a sprawling heap. There was a flurry of shots around and over him, a searing rush of lead grazing his upper arm, another close enough to his ear to almost deafen him, and then he was scrambling to his feet, the Winchester already blazing like a fiery torch, spraying shots across anything that had a shape and moved.

It was a full half-minute before Cavendish came to realize that he was still standing, still alive, and faced now by the sole remaining Apache. His trigger finger reacted instinctively on the advancing target, only to feel the dull, dead thud as the action jammed.

The buck needed no telling, no better incentive then to spring forward, his own rifle lifting for the single shot that would down the marshal before an eye had blinked.

Cavendish flung himself to his left, scrambled, rushed, kicked sand, heard the mare snorting and prancing at his back, then, swinging the rifle to a barrel grip, dashed at the Apache like a man in a frenzy of fever.

He felt the butt make contact as the Apache's shot ranged high and wide, was conscious of a deep groan, a rattle of throttled breath, a last, bewildered gasp behind a sudden silence before he collapsed at the side of Ellie Gates's bruised, unmoving body.

She looked to be more dead than alive.

Fourteen

Brenton Clewes drew all five-feet-four of him to his full height, adjusted the drape of his frock coat, settled his hat, examined the shine on his boots, checked his timepiece and helped himself to another finger of whiskey.

Rough quality, he grimaced, thudding the empty glass to the side table, not a patch on eastern blends, but then no more than he would expect of a frontier town like Eldron. Just about everything hereabouts was rough: rough food, rough drink, rough folk – damnit, even the hotel beds were rough!

He grunted, squinted at the half-empty bottle and poured another measure. What the hell, a fellow had to make the most of the hand dealt. No point in getting critical, not at a time like this. Nossir, too far down the trail now, too much at stake. What were a few days of frontier inconvenience against the lush living to come? Nothing, not a bag of nails. Why, a hundred fellows would give an arm for his prospects, and gladly so.

He sniffed, sipped at the drink and crossed to the window overlooking the dusty main street. Godforsaken heap of a settlement if ever he had seen one. Two-bit folk clinging to new lands' hope, drifters with no better place to drift to, the lost, the lonely, no-hopers and has-beens, some already drained, most getting that way. Rough, no other word for it.

But the sheriff was smart. Was he! Not the sort by a mile you would expect in a town like Eldron. No, Frank Church was young, strong, sharp thinking and good-looking with it. Too capable by far this distance West. Should have been back East some place – and he half-wished right now he was just that. Still, he was only one, and one alone, and would be no problem when the time came.

Meanwhile, put the fellow to good use, that was the trick of it. Keep him busy, involved, make him *seem* important. All part of the strategy and planning, and he, Brenton Augustus Clewes, was the master of strategy bar none. He was the man of ideas, vision, the 'thinker' who could plot and scheme to the finest detail, so that come show-down, come the day, nothing had been overlooked, not a thread, not a stitch in the grand pattern. That was the real Brenton Clewes: master tactician, manipulator of the shadows.

He finished the drink in a single gulp, replaced

the glass and consulted his timepiece again. Sheriff would be here in ten minutes. Time enough to mull the plan over for any cracks and be sure all was as it should be. But it would. Of course it would. It was *his* plan!

Brenton Clewes smiled softly to himself and stiffened to his five-feet-four again. Odd, he mused, how tall a man could get if he thought about it for long enough.

'Way I see it, Mr Clewes, yuh got nothin' to fret over. Looks to be tight as a sleepin' tick and buttoned down. Yuh can relax.'

Sheriff Frank Church turned his hat through his long, slim fingers and smiled almost condescendingly at the spruce, twitchy fellow standing at the window of the shadowed room.

Not every day Eldron played host to the likes of Brenton Clewes, he was thinking, watching the man flick nervously at specks of dust on the lapels of his coat. But he guessed the nerves were to be expected. Damn it, the fellow was sure as hell shouldering some responsibility, $30,000 worth of it, give or take a few hundreds either way. Not the sort of burden a fellow slept easy with. Hardly surprising he was a mite twitchy, so would he be if he was personally responsible for a shipment of gold of that order reaching its destination safely – which in one sense he was, at least as far as the Eldron end of the operation was concerned.

Sooner it was over the easier he would feel.

'Appreciate your reassurance,' said Clewes, picking at a particularly annoying speck, 'and I admire your confidence. Can't say fairer, Sheriff. Always the first to acknowledge confidence. Yessir. Comes of a lifetime in banking, you understand. Don't get to be president of the Eastern Federal for nothin', you know. Takes insight, mister. The ability to read a fellow, like you would a book. Understand the character, the motivation, the plot. Know what I mean?'

'Well, I guess—' began Church.

' 'Course you do,' grinned Clewes. 'Smart fellow as you are. Knew it the minute I clapped eyes on you. Said to m'self, now here's a fella to be trusted. Fine, upstanding man of the law, I said. No foolin' this fella, and won't stand for no messin' neither. Very reassurin', given the delicacy of the operation.'

'Yuh can bet—' began Church again.

'Oh, I'm no bettin' man,' said Clewes, linking his hands behind him. 'Never bet on anythin', mister – 'ceptin', of course, when *I've* selected the field and set the odds!' The grin flickered again. 'Certainties. I only bet on certainties, and you, Sheriff Church, are a certainty. Can see it on your face.'

'Just doin' my job,' smiled the sheriff.

'And very efficient too. Highly satisfactory. But just so we're in no doubt, and to be sure there's nothin' we've overlooked, shall we run through the plannin' one more time? Bankin' habit, you understand. Check and double check. Now—'

'As I understand it,' said Church, stifling an irritated sigh, 'there's two wagons been trailin' these past ten days outa the gold strike at Nagaro. First big shipment since the company out there got lucky. Close on a value of thirty thousand dollars.' He paused. 'Some haul,' he added thoughtfully. 'Bankers to the company are the Eastern Federal, of which you, sir, are first president.'

'Correct,' murmured Clewes.

'There's a dozen company men ridin' shotgun with the shipment on its trail to a final destination at the bank in Wichita. But meantime there'll be a change over of guards right here in Eldron. Company replaced by bank men, they bein' on their way here right now, due to hit town in forty-eight hours, same time as the shipment. Wagons'll be here one full day before pullin' out East. You, Mr Clewes, will be ridin' along of them. And yuh here now to see that all goes as it should on the last leg of the journey.'

'Excellent,' beamed Clewes. 'And your role in all this, Sheriff?'

'Yuh askin' me to ensure the safety of the shipment while it over-nights here and provision yuh men and horses accordingly. No problem. I got a coupla good deputies and there's fellas hereabouts

who'll be glad enough to earn a few dollars for
stayin' awake. Yuh don't have to worry, sir, not one
bit.'

'I'm sure I don't,' smiled Clewes, 'and you'll find
the Eastern Federal more than generous in
return for your help. But there is just one point
comes to mind, Mr Church, small and irrelevant,
perhaps, but a point nonetheless.'

'That bein'?'

'That bein' the possibility of, how shall I say,
ambush, hi-jack? Unlikely, no doubt, but it pays to
consider all eventualities. I'm thinkin' of the trail
the shipment is takin' as we speak. That safe
enough, in your opinion, Sheriff?'

'Trail from Nagaro to Eldron is as safe as any.
Ain't never heard of no trouble along it.'

'And doesn't the Drinkwater Drift trail reach it
some place?'

'Sure it does,' grinned Church, 'few miles north
of here, but the Drift's the least of yuh worries.
Ain't nobody tackles the Drinkwater, not unless
he's lookin' to an early death! Nothin' comes outa
the Drift, Mr Clewes, save crawlin' skin and bone.
And that's a fact.'

'Good,' beamed Clewes again, 'then we have
nothin' to fear. All is well, on time and just as it
should be. Only remains for me to remind you,
Sheriff, of the need for the utmost discretion. No
loose talk of the shipment, or indeed of my pres-
ence here.'

'Understood,' grunted Church.

'Excellent. And now I think I might rest a while until supper. Perhaps you will join me, Mr Church, assumin' there's somewhere we might dine?'

Brenton Clewes spent the few hours to dusk in quiet contemplation of his planning. It was good, complete and neat, no loose ends, no ill-fitting joints, and he had the added bonus now of the sheriff under control. Excellent. Almost too good. But, no, perhaps not. This, after all, was a Brenton Clewes's operation and therefore sure to be sound. All it needed was for the last piece of the plan to slip into place.

No trouble there either: he had always been able to rely on Moses Ratrap.

Fifteen

Only one thing about the smooth-talking banker out of Wichita troubled Sheriff Frank Church: how come Brenton Clewes was here alone?

How was it the first president of the Eastern Federal had no sidekicks looking to his safety and well-being? Why did a fellow that important, that wealthy, choose to travel alone on a mission involving a fortune in gold? Had he ridden all the way from the bank's headquarters without so much as a lick of luggage, without an escort, with nothing, it seemed, save what he stood in?

How come, when you really got to thinking on it deep and straight enough, a fellow as fussy about his appearance as Brenton Clewes holed-up in a place like Eldron with only one pair of boots and no change of shirt?

Damn it, thought Church, turning the lantern light in his office to a soft, midnight glow, it was that sort of thinking that could land a lawman in a whole heap of embarrassing hot water. Nobody

got to questioning the motives, personal or profes-
sional, of a fellow of the standing of Brenton
Clewes, not unless he was hell-bent on taking to a
hermit's life in the hills.

Nobody did, nobody would — save somebody
with the fool curiosity of Frank Church. But, then,
nobody in Eldron save the sheriff had taken
supper with the banker and been close enough to
notice that the cuffs of the man's tailored shirt
had been as grimy and dirt-stained as the day he
had ridden in.

But, hell, did it matter? Few in Eldron had ever
seen a clean shirt, let alone owned more than the
one they were wearing. So maybe Brenton Clewes
was simply merging unnoticed into the local
colour, passing, so he figured, for an ordinary
fellow.

Even so, for a man who picked every last speck
of dust from his fancy frock coat, he was a mite
careless over his shirt cuffs. As for being here
alone, well, who was to know how the first president of a bank got to thinking? Fellows of the cut
of Brenton Clewes were a law unto themselves.

But not in Eldron.

No, thought Church, taking another turn round
his cramped, shadow-shared office, the law was
Colorado law in Eldron and would stay that way.
Sheriff would do his duty, *by the law*, and that was
the sum of it.

That gold shipment out of Nagaro would arrive

and be suitably guarded; company outriders and bank fellows would be fed and watered, as would the horses, and when the time came for the laden wagons to pull out that would be that. The gold at that point would be the responsibility of Brenton Clewes and his men, every last mile to Wichita, come what may.

First president's shirt cuffs would sure as hell be scuffed black as crows by then!

Church stretched, yawned and collected his Winchester from the rifle rack. Time to take a last turn through town, he figured, make sure the place was sleeping as it should, give himself some quiet space to think through the shipment arrangements.

Damn it, why Eldron, he wondered? Why all that gold in a dead-beat town where even the dust got turned only once a year? Took some figuring.

Slow curl of smoke at the livery; soft snort from an irritable mount back of Jonesey's store; hound whimpering home to an empty barn; giggle through an open window above the saloon; light still burning there in Clewes's room.

Fellow stayed up late, thought Church, holding to the shadows on the boardwalk opposite. Maybe he was checking out the plan again, looking for the loopholes that might lead to ambush. Hell, he was a whole forest of planks short in his reckoning on a danger coming out of the Drinkwater!

111

Not been so much as a rider from that quarter since gun-slinging Joe Drummond made a dash for it two years back, and they never did find his bones. Mr Clewes might know his banking, but he had some way to go to understanding territory.

Could be, of course, mused Church, giving the light a last glance, that the fellow was scrubbing up his shirt-cuffs!

He smiled softly to himself, paused a moment to scan the other windows, nodded to the girl, taking in the air from a top room, winced at the grab from behind that pulled her back to the darkness, and strolled on.

Quiet night in Eldron, much as it always was, he thought, stepping from the last of the board-walk to the dirt. Most action he might see between now and first light would be a rowdy drunk, a girl scuttling half-naked from one of the fringe line of shacks where the drifters holed-up, maybe a brawl back of one of them, some lonely-eyed trail woman offering to sell herself for the price of a half-empty bottle. . . .

One of these days he might throw in the badge at Eldron and go get himself some real action in one of them gambling towns back East; some place that never slept, was always humming with life and the crazy characters peopling it. Who could say, he might get to being a marshal in polished boots, cut pants and jacket, bone-white shirt-cuffs stiff as board, with a bank account at

the Eastern Federal! Now that would surely be—
He halted, suddenly tense, at the slow, eerie creak of leather, the jangle of worn tack, scuff of tired hoofs.

It was a full minute before Sheriff Frank Church had any shapes to the approaching sounds.

He was sweating by then, conscious of the tight persistent prickle at the back of his neck, a sensation he had not felt in months and never in Eldron at a half-past midnight. Nobody, but nobody, not even the worst of loose-headed drifters, rode in at this hour, not through a darkness that, once settled in these parts, all but left a fellow damn near blind.

But somebody was riding in this night, sure enough, somebody in no hurry, at no pace, on a mount struggling to put one hoof ahead of the next, that might be moving more by instinct than intent.

First recognizable shape Church had in his fixed, narrowed gaze was the man slumped close to exhaustion across the mount's neck. There was a dazed, glazed look in the fellow's eyes as his head rolled to the slow, plodding pace; hands loose and lifeless on the reins, legs dangling like the limbs of a worn marionette, his whole frame threatening to topple to the ground at the next step.

But the sweat in the sheriff's neck chilled to a

113

trickle of ice at the sight of the shape trailing on a loose line to the mount at the man's back. A woman, or what there was of her that resembled anything female, her face sun-scorched, blistered, the eyes set like black holes in her head, hair dripping like bleached weed to the rough blanket covering her body. White woman; Apache pony. Hell, just what, how in God's name. . . .

'Water,' croaked the man, and slid from the mount to the dirt without another sound.

Sixteen

'Yuh askin' me to swallow a whole mouthful of possibilities there, Marshal, and with respect and bearin' in mind—'

'Respect be damned, mister! We're countin' down the hours to a bloodbath! Ain't yuh got that yet?' Sam Cavendish crashed the mug to the table in the sheriff's dimly lit office and watched the spilled coffee spread like a dark lake. He waited a moment, ran a hand over his dirt-stained face and stubble, sighed and leaned back in the chair. 'Sorry. I ain't fixin' for a shoutin' match with yuh,' he murmured. 'Grateful to yuh for sortin' us out like yuh have, but gettin' to be all-in.'

'Yuh been all-in for hours,' said Church, mopping a rag through the spillage. 'Yuh need to sleep, same as the woman there.' He nodded to the cell where the door stood open on the sleeping form of Ellie Gates. 'She's all-in, sure enough. Damned lucky to be alive. How she came through—'

'She's a survivor, mister,' sighed Cavendish. 'Take more than a bunch of maraudin' Apaches to knock the life outa her. She's got good reasons to stay breathin'. A murdered husband bein' only one of 'em.'

'Well, mebbe,' said Church, seating himself opposite the marshal, 'but that's another matter. 'More to the point—'

'More to the point is what you're goin' to do about Moses Ratrap once he's in position to hit that gold shipment. That's the *point*, Sheriff.'

'Look,' said Church, leaning forward, his arms flat on the table, 'I ain't got reason to doubt that what Mrs Gates has told yuh is right – it all adds up now, don't it, with what I've told yuh about that fella Clewes we got holed-up here? – but, hell, Marshal, I ain't in no position to go hit Ratrap. Just ain't got the manpower, not shootin' men, I ain't. Aside of my two deputies, who ain't no great shakes savin' when it comes to handlin' drunks, most of the scumbags hereabouts are just that, scumbags. Don't think a deal beyond saloon times and gettin' their quota. Best plan I got, it seems, is go tell Clewes what you and the lady there have come across and get m'self out to that shipment. Stop it right where it is until we either get to Ratrap or raise some respectable guns. Lord above knows where.'

Cavendish drummed his fingers on the table, grunted and settled a tired gaze on the sheriff.

'This fella Clewes,' he murmured, 'yuh trust him?'

'Hell, he is first president of the Eastern Federal! 'Course I trust him. Wouldn't you? That gold shipment out there is big even by his standards. Last thing he wants is for anythin' to happen to it. That's why he's here, protectin' his interests.'

Cavendish grunted. 'And alone,' he murmured again.

'Like I told yuh, Marshal, that does trouble me some, but when yuh happen to be first president. . . . Hell, he don't take orders from nobody, does he? Just hands 'em out and makes his own rules.'

Cavendish's fingers came to rest and his gaze drifted into the shadowed space. 'I been trailin' Moses Ratrap for what seems like a lifetime, 'til I know how he thinks, when he thinks it, why he thinks it. I know exactly what he's capable of, and there ain't a pit that deep the sonofabitch won't bottom out to stay alive and feedin' his greed – ask Mrs Gates – but I'll tell yuh somethin', Sheriff, that rat don't shift a muscle of his butt 'til he's got some scheme sorted that's laced tighter than a preacher-wife's bodice. Fact, mister, plain fact.'

The marshal's gaze narrowed. 'When I'd finally got some life back into Mrs Gates and she was up to tellin' me what Farrars had spilled in his haste about the gold and the urgency of gettin' to

117

Eldron, first thing I asked m'self was, how come Ratrap knew about the gold, what was it made him so certain he was goin' to lift it to risk the Drinkwater Drift draggin' his own army along of him – every one of his whores bein' good shots, yuh can bet – and just who had paid for and supplied them spankin' new Winchesters?' His gaze flashed like a light to Church's face. 'Any ideas, mister?'

'What yuh sayin', Marshal?'

'Work it out while I get some rest.' Cavendish came wearily to his feet. 'Lady there and me sure scorched some dirt gettin' here, but skirtin' Ratrap's outfits was no problem. Lucky we rounded up a pony for Mrs Gates, but she could use some clean clothes when she wakes. Mebbe yuh could fix it, nice and quiet, eh? Don't want nobody to know we're in town, so keep that door locked.' He turned to the cell, paused and turned again. 'Give me a coupla hours. First light. No longer. There ain't the time. Oh, and keep an eye on that first president. But don't tell him nothin'. Not a thing.'

Sheriff Frank Church had waited just long enough for the marshal to settle himself and slide into a deep, sonorous sleep before slipping softly from the office, locking the door behind him and passing silently into the street's night shadows.

Hell, not two hours back he had been bemoaning the shortage of action in town! Now, if he was to follow the thinking of Sam Cavendish, Eldron was all set to become a border-town hell-hole, centrepiece to what would probably pass into history as one of the biggest – and maybe bloodiest – gold heists of all time.

Some action!

He wiped a new lathering of sweat from his neck, took a long, deep breath and relaxed. Well, he pondered, did he follow the marshal's thinking; was this town, of all towns, about to put itself on the map of legend, and was that smooth-talking, frock-coated banker, Brenton Clewes, the linchpin in the whole grisly business? If he was, how was he, a small-time sheriff in a two-bit, no-hoper town, going to handle it?

And even if Clewes was innocent of any conspiracy, there was still the threat of Moses Ratrap and his 'army' moving in from the Drift. So how was he going to handle that?

Damn it, he needed men, and he needed guns, fast! Best he could muster would be a handful of old soaks and two greenhorn deputies. From there on, it would, sure as fate, be history – his own writ small on a Boot Hill marker!

'Hell,' he muttered, clearing more sweat, stiffening to his full height, then moving away down the dark, empty street.

Action he had wanted, action he had surely got!

119

*

There was still a light in the back room of O'Hara's Saloon when Church reached the door, paused a moment, tapped lightly and passed without being beckoned into the gloomy den of the proprietor.

'Can't sleep, Sheriff, or just gettin' an early start?' grinned the owner, coming to his feet from the chair at a roll-top desk. 'Me, I never sleep! What's yuh problem? Use a drink?'

'No, thanks,' said Church, leaning against the door jamb. 'Just checkin' round.'

'Mite late, ain't it? Only checkin' yuh need at this hour is to check who's in whose bed!' Clem O'Hara stepped to a side cabinet and poured a finger of whiskey. 'Or yuh got somebody special in mind?' he smiled, from behind the glass.

'That fella I supped with t'night, Brenton Clewes. He abed?' asked Church.

'Ain't been out of it since yuh left,' said O'Hara, finishing the drink with a wince then a slap of his lips. 'Darn stuff. Gut-rot!' He replaced the empty glass and hooked his thumbs in his waistcoat. 'Sure he has. Annie seen to that!'

'Annie?' frowned the sheriff.

'No less. Yuh imagine that – fella standin' no higher than a short boot with a gal like Annie, six-feet-two if she's an inch! Still, she was the one he wanted. Asked for her soon after yuh'd gone. And

120

we're here to oblige. Ain't no law against it. Paid well too. And yuh know somethin', Sheriff, fella said to Annie as how he was real taken with her and would she like to hitch along of him when he pulls out.'

'That so?' murmured Church, twitching his shoulders against a trickle of sweat. 'He say when he might be pullin' out?'

'Coupla days.'

'Takes all sorts,' shrugged Church. 'How's Annie feel about headin' Wichita way?'

'Wichita?' croaked O'Hara. 'Fella didn't say nothin' about Wichita. No, he wants to take Annie to Mexico, clean across the border to some *hacienda* hideout. Yuh figure Annie for a *señorita*, Sheriff?'

Church stayed silent, his thoughts running like a stampede.

'Say, just who is this fella Clewes, anyhow?' asked O'Hara, pouring another drink. 'He some big-shot from Mexico way? Got himself some spread down there? What's he doin' in a godforsaken dump like this? Yuh got any idea, Sheriff?'

'Mebbe,' murmured Church as he left O'Hara to his drink and slid back to the night.

Seventeen

Ellie Gates ran her fingers down the cold smoothness of the cell bars and wondered if this had been her real and only destiny since the night of the shooting back in Duncan?

Joe's fear and obsessions had been a cell in which they had both been imprisoned. The Drift and Moses Ratrap had been a prison, and she had been a prisoner of the marauding Apaches, so maybe a cell in a lost border town she had never even heard of was just another along the line. Only difference being that the door to this cell stood open and she could walk out anytime she chose.

If she had the courage. . . .

'Feelin' better?' asked Cavendish, stepping from the table to the cell.

'Do I look it?' said Ellie.

'Not a deal, ma'am,' murmured the marshal. 'Clothes look good, though. Sheriff rounded 'em up from some place.'

Drift Raiders

Ellie smiled softly and ran a hand over the clean shirt and buckskin skirt. 'I'm grateful. Feels a whole lot better.' She sighed quietly. 'Yourself, Mr Cavendish? How are you? Don't answer. I can see.' She sighed again. 'T'ain't over, is it? Not by a long shot.' Her grip on the bars tightened. 'Any news of Ratrap? You told the sheriff about the gold? What about—?'

'Steady on there, ma'am. Don't go racin' ahead of y'self. Yuh ain't in no fit state.'

'A *fit state* is somethin' I ain't been in for a long time, but that ain't of no account. What matters is—'

'I'll tell yuh what matters, Mrs Gates,' snapped Cavendish. 'What matters is you stayin' safe and gettin' y'self back to feelin' somethin' like human again. Sheriff's got that in hand. There's a place—'

'If yuh think for one minute yuh goin' to shove me away in some corner—'

'No, ma'am, that I ain't doin'. Wouldn't rate, I know that. No, yuh goin' to work. We got a job for yuh. There's a fella holed-up at the saloon, name of Brenton Clewes, who I figure to be. . . . Well, I'll go into that later. Your job is goin' to be stayin' real close so yuh don't lose sight of him for one second. Won't be easy, but yuh wouldn't want it no other.'

'And you – what'll you be doin' while I'm fawning in Mr Clewes's shadow?'

'Sheriff and me'll be—'

The door to the office flew open under the whirling rush of Frank Church. 'We got a sight of him!' he croaked, one hand on the door. 'At the Drift, sun-up. Sent my best deputy out there. Just got back. Says Ratrap and his wagons'll clear the Drinkwater in an hour. So what'll we do?' He glanced hurriedly at Ellie Gates. 'Oh, 'mornin', ma'am. Glad to see yuh up. Sorry about—'

'Get my horse, Sheriff,' snapped Cavendish. 'And as many guns as yuh can raise. Then we ride – and you, ma'am, shift that pretty butt and get to work!'

Ellie blinked on wide eyes, opened her mouth to speak, but said nothing as she stepped from the cell.

They swirled the early morning trail dust to high, drifting clouds as they cleared the town of Eldron and headed into the bleak lands fronting the mouth of the Drinkwater Drift.

They were five strong: Marshal Sam Cavendish, Sheriff Frank Church, two deputies and the only drifter in town sober enough to mount a horse and strap a gun. Hardly a menacing threat to deter Moses Ratrap from his intended attack on the shipment, thought Cavendish, narrowing his gaze against the dust clouds, but the best that time and the town could muster.

124

'No pause for fineries, Mr Church,' he had told the sheriff as they hit the trail. 'Keep it simple. Split one of yuh men west to the Nagaro trail to halt them gold wagons right where he finds 'em. Rest of us find Ratrap and stay close 'til we know precisely where he's goin' and what he's plannin'.'

'Only one thing on his mind,' Church had offered, 'and that's hittin' the shipment hard and fast as he can. *That* simple, Mr Cavendish.'

'Yuh don't know Ratrap,' Cavendish had called against the thud of hoofs. 'He don't do nothin' by any man's logic. Figure the impossible, and that's Moses, bet yuh boots on it.'

'We ain't got nothin' like enough guns, and no hope of raisin' 'em. Can't take on—'

'Don't get to worryin' yet, Mr Church. We got the time for that when it's starin' us full on.'

'That woman goin' to be safe back there?' Church had asked.

'Mister, yuh can rest easy. Brenton Clewes ain't goin' no place or doin' nothin' from here on that Ellie Gates won't know about. Spider and fly – no odds on who's which!'

'Hell, I just don't—'

'Ride, Mr Church. Just ride!'

They were an hour down the trail with the grey sprawl of the Drinkwater crags in sight and about to let the chosen deputy cut loose for the shipment, when the sweat in Sheriff Church's neck ran suddenly chiller and tighter at the sight of the slow curl of smoke to the cloudless sky a mile distant.

He called a warning to Cavendish and pointed ahead.

'I see it, mister,' shouted the marshal without breaking pace as he veered the mare into rougher ground. Sure he did, he thought, spitting dust from his lips, saw the smoke clear enough but could make about as much sense of it in those first moments as he could Ratrap's twisted thinking. What the hell, the sonofabitch got to burning wagons or something, gone completely out of his mind? Or had he. . . .

But it was too late by then for the marshal's reckoning on the reason for the curl of smoke to turn to action. Too late, but not quite late enough for that first whining crack of a Winchester to split his skull. Cavendish had lowered himself instinctively to the mount's neck at the thought of a trap. He heard, could almost feel the shot sear above his head as he realized that somebody among Ratrap's followers must have spotted Church's lone deputy pinpointing them at dawn. That would have been all Ratrap needed to settle an insurance against prying eyes: lure the curious to you; never give them time to figure the web. But Cavendish had, by no more than a whisker.

'To yuh left!' he yelled at the top of his voice. 'The boulders! Make for the boulders!'

He was conscious of Church's mount skidding

alongside him as more shots cracked and whined,
saw the drifter thrown from his saddle like blown
brush, blood spouting from his neck, the leading
deputy's horse panic and lose its foothold in a
twisting veil of dust, the rider already lifeless
where he hung by a foot caught in a stirrup.

Damn it, whoever it was behind the
Winchesters in the crags at the Drift had the
benefit of deep cover and would pick their targets
off at leisure in open land. Cavendish slung
himself still lower to the mare's neck and urged
her forward, catching no more than a blurred
glimpse of Church as his mount snorted through
flying sweat.

The second deputy had almost reached the line
of boulders when a single, roaring shot threw him
from his horse to a twitching mass in the dirt.
'Hell!' screamed Church, and in one thrusting
leap had urged his mount clear of the body and
flung himself headlong into the rocks.

Cavendish was in the man's shadow as he
crashed, gasping and choking, dirt-smeared and
sweat-stained to the deputy's side.

'Of all the sonofabitch—' spluttered Church.

'Save yuh breath,' croaked the marshal. 'T'ain't
no time for cursin'.'

'How many guns out there? Damn it, we ain't
got a soul left savin' ourselves. I lost good men
there, yuh know that? To hell with that sonofabitch! And just where the hell is Ratrap?'

'I'll tell yuh just where he ain't,' groaned Cavendish, slumping against a boulder as the last of the gunfire echoed to silence. 'He ain't in the Drift no more. He spotted that deputy yuh sent out, let him ride free, then sprung all this in the certainty that some fool-heads would come hell-raisin' out here – and we did, Mr Church, yessir, we did just that! That's Ratrap thinkin' for yuh.' He spat a mouthful of dirt. 'Wager a year's pay he broke open them crated Winchesters, used the timber for the fire and left three fellas here to pick off whoever happened along. Simple as that.'

'And where's the rat now?' winced Church, rubbing his shoulders. 'Yuh figured that?'

'Right now he's halfway to Eldron, all set to meet with his benefactor, Brenton Clewes, and wait for that shipment rollin' to his doorstep.'

'Make the robbery right there in town, f'Crissake?' groaned Church.

'Where better? With the law outa town and the bank's first president there in person to welcome the shipment, what could be easier?'

'Hell!' moaned the sheriff. 'Hell! So how we goin'—?'

'Them guns out there are fixin' on pinnin' us down 'til they get a chance to move in. But they're goin' to get impatient, real itchy at the thought of all that gold bein' shared out there in town. They'll move sooner than they should – and we'll be waitin'.'

128

'Waitin'?' frowned Church. 'We just goin' to sit here and wait to get killed?'

'No, Mr Church, not that simple. We'll be doin' the killin' this time, and then ridin' like hell – into the teeth of it!'

Eighteen

Brenton Clewes rolled his timepiece through his sweaty hand, consulted it again and placed it carefully, face up, on the table in front of him. Another two hours, he thought, perhaps a mite less before the curtain went up on 'the show'.

He smiled softly to himself. He supposed it was a 'show' of a type, a colourful spread of pure theatre, expertly plotted and staged with an ingenious last act and a twist in the tail. Only trouble was, he frowned, some of the characters were no longer 'waiting in the wings'.

Just where, for instance, was that young sheriff? Certainly not in town. Where were his deputies, and why was there a sudden air of tension about the place? It had not been there last night. Sheriff Church had been relaxed, easy speaking, at ease, untroubled, doubtless glad of the chance to take supper in a heap like Eldron with someone as important as a first president of the Eastern Federal, even though the steaks had been a touch aged. A minor detail.

It had been a peaceful, convivial evening concluding on more than a note of extreme satisfaction once that long-legged Annie had got to the drift of his thinking. . . . Indeed. He must do something about her future, he reminded himself. She was wasted in O'Hara's Saloon.

But today, this morning, here at a secluded table in a corner of the bar, with an unrestricted view of the comings and goings, things were different.

No sheriff, no O'Hara, not a sight of the girl – only the drunks getting into harness for the day, the staring, moon-eyed drifters, the uninterested barman, a strangely muted hum to the conversation, a sticky, airless heat, the feel of dust hanging like webs.

And the woman.

Yes, thought Clewes, the woman. She was still there, other side of the batwings, passing quietly to and fro along the boardwalk, pausing to glance into the bar, moving on, turning, coming back. Same steady pace, same incisive glance. Back and forth for close on an hour.

Why, he wondered? She waiting for somebody? Looking for somebody? She was a cut above the average Eldron female. Touch of class in the way she held her head and moved. Confident, assured, woman who knew her status and stood to it. No

131

hanger-on to scumbag drifters. Nossir. There would be no stale trail dust packing her skirts!

But he would wager she was a stranger in town. Not been here yesterday or last night. So who was she, where had she come from and when and just who had been at her side?

Clewes consulted his timepiece again and tapped a finger thoughtfully on the table. He had the time, he decided, and certainly the inclination, so why not? No harm done in making the woman's acquaintance. A pleasant diversion. Take his mind off the 'show'. Damn it, he had rehearsed it often enough!

He waited until the woman paused at the batwings again, caught her eye, raised his hat and smiled.

Curtain up!

Marshal Cavendish cleared the lather of sweat from his face, eased the Winchester to his side and nodded to Sheriff Church.

'Yuh reckon?' hissed Church from the shadow of the boulders.

Cavendish held up a hand and spread the fingers, then slid like a lizard to the far side of the cover. He was gambling, damn it, he knew that. Maybe the sidekicks were in no hurry, after all; content enough to sit it out, wait for the sun and the heat to take their toll. Maybe they were under

Ratrap's orders to do just that, and would, without question, given a normal situation. But this was about as normal as petting a side-winder. This involved gold, a whole heap of it, and men had neither sense of duty nor obligation when a gold share-out was in the reckoning. They went their own way, fast as they could.

He blinked, grunted and took in what he could see between a narrow gap in the boulders. Bodies, blood, gathering flies, a drifting buzzard, a stray mount standing lost and bewildered. He grunted again. Sorry sight, about as nerve-grinding as it got. And it showed sure as hell in the sheriff's face; that look of despair, disgust, anger. Maybe it had been his first experience of a real shooting to kill or be killed. Well, he was learning fast, and the lessons were a long way from being over.

Cavendish eased back, checked that Church was still alert and primed and squirmed over the hot sand to come face-on to where Ratrap's men were holed-up.

The curl of smoke was no more now than a faint finger to the high blue, the only movement over the deserted land; the silence hung empty and waiting, almost twitching, it seemed, at a buzzing fly.

'Anythin'?' hissed Church.

'Soon enough,' murmured Cavendish. 'Yuh gettin' impatient or somethin'?'

'Just thinkin' what I'd like to do once I get my hands on them sonsofbitches. Figurin' how long I could make it last before—'

The crack of the shot came ahead of the pound and scuff of boots through dirt. Another, clipping the surface of a boulder, sent a shower of sparks and chippings over the marshal's shoulders.

'They're comin' head-on!' croaked Church.

'Let 'em,' snarled Cavendish. 'Hold yuh fire and let 'em! Scumbags are fazed with gold fever!'

More shots now, high, wild and swinging. Boots kicking dirt. A yell, a shout splitting the morning apart, until, just when it seemed to Church that the marshal had left it too late, was too slow, that Ratrap's men would over-run them, Cavendish rose in the boulders like some suddenly threatening cloud, the Winchester blazing from his hip, his whole body tensed to a fighting machine that sprayed lead as if that same cloud had crashed to a storm.

Church was at his side in an instant, his Colt levelled, steady, roaring fire, gaze narrowed in anger as he watched the three sidekicks thrown high and back and finally to the dirt like flotsam swept through a flood tide.

'Nice work, Sheriff,' murmured Cavendish, shouldering the Winchester through a slow grin. 'Fellas just couldn't wait, could they? No patience. No damn patience!' He spat, eased the sweat from his neck and grunted. 'Now let's go find ourselves

134

some real action, eh? Let's go singe Ratrap's mean stubble!'

You bet, thought Church. You just bet on it!

'Like I always say, my dear,' smiled Brenton Clewes, smoothing his fingers over the back of Ellie Gates's hand, 'a lady of taste and class is deservin' of only the best, the finest money can buy. And I, ma'am, have money, and to spare.'

Ellie stifled the shiver at her spine, relaxed her hand on the table and leaned forward invitingly. 'Well, now, Mr Clewes,' she purred, 'that really is a compliment, 'specially so out here, in a town like this, where there just don't seem the space—'

'I understand, my dear, understand completely, and if you'll just be patient a while 'til I got my business here finished, why, we got the whole world waitin' as an oyster. And that, ma'am, is a fact.' Clewes's smile deepened. 'Must be my lucky day, and some!'

Ellie shifted the hand a gentle fraction. 'Mine too, I guess,' she whispered, her eyes gleaming. 'Do hope this business ain't goin' to take long. I got no hankerin' for stayin' in this town longer than's necessary.'

'A few hours,' hummed Clewes. 'Just a few short hours, my dear.'

Ellie pouted theatrically. 'That long? I was wonderin', kinda hopin'—'

'Soon as my partners are here and the . . .

135

transactions completed, we'll be on our way. I promise.'

'Meantime?' pouted Ellie again.

'Meantime, ma'am, another drink, eh, time for you to tell me all about yourself? Why we hardly had the time to exchange more than names, have we, and there's so much about you I'd like to know.'

'Yuh would?' smiled Ellie. 'Really?'

'Sure, I would. All there is.'

'Well, in that case,' said Ellie, slipping the hand from beneath Clewes's fingers, 'why don't we go discuss it? Some place quiet? Private? Your room, Mr Clewes? If yuh got the time, that is.'

Brenton Clewes came to his full five-feet-four, collected his timepiece and without giving it a second glance, slid it to his pocket.

Nineteen

Moses Ratrap pushed a defiant hand at the brim of his floppy hat, let a long, soft grin swim over his sweat-streaked face, and waited for the dust to settle.

This far and now this close, he mused, beginning to hum quietly through his heavy, dirt-crusted breathing. This close . . . no more than a half-hour's drive to the first of the blurred shapes that were the town of Eldron. Be there long before noon. Have the whole operation in place and waiting in an hour, and then. . . . Then it would be like taking candy from a jar. Easy as that, no problem.

He relaxed the reins and let the horses stand. Rest up a while, give them a breather. Just sit here, taking in them shapes, that town, the pot of gold at the end of the trail.

'Yuh want me to go check on the boys back there?' called Goose Farrars, reining his outfit alongside Ratrap.

'No need,' murmured the old man vaguely, his

gaze still on the shapes, reins loose in his lap. 'They knew what to do.'

'Mebbe,' said Goose, 'but that ain't to say they did it.'

'Yuh heard the shootin'. Ain't that enough?'

Goose hawked and spat. 'Seems a mite strange to me. Kinda chills.' He rolled his shoulders as if shrugging off some invisible touch. 'How come that fella rode out, anyhow? What brought him outa town to the Drift at that hour? Weren't there for his health.'

'Don't matter none, does it?' said Ratrap, still gazing. 'Boys would've taken care of whoever the fella went to fetch. That's why I let him go. Get the decks cleared. Cut out the curious.'

'Yuh figure it for that – curiosity? That simple?'

'That simple,' grinned Ratrap. 'Tell yuh somethin', Goose, somethin' yuh should have a mind to. We got the best brain there is bar none workin' for us there in town. The fella that put this whole operation t'gether. Did yuh know that? Well, mebbe not, eh, mebbe yuh had no idea, not so much as a grain of one, that we, Goose, have the first president of the Eastern Federal, no less, sittin' right there in Eldron pullin' all the strings on our behalf. Yuh imagine that? The first president. Now him and me go back some, way back, and I can tell yuh for absolute certainty, on the Good Book, friend, that a first president don't make mistakes. Not one.

That's why he's first president. See?'

Goose grunted. 'Well . . .' he muttered.

'Now that first president,' Ratrap went on, 'will have had the sheriff there in Eldron tight in his pocket from the minute he hit town, and there ain't nothin', not a snitch, not a sneeze that same first president won't know to. So, if some fella rides out, sees us at the Drift and rides back, our man, our first president, would know. I'll wager, Goose, real heavy, that our man mebbe *organized* it so's the sheriff himself would come high-tailin' to the Drinkwater and our boys could take him out. Yeah, I would at that. Sorta thing he would do. Bet yuh there ain't a stitch of law in that godforsaken town when we ride in. Nossir, not a stitch! Don't the Good Lord work in mysterious ways? Don't He just! Hallelujah!'

Goose spat again. 'If yuh so say, Moses,' he muttered.

'I do, I do, my friend. Now let's get to buttonin' matters, eh? Way I see it from here, there's a livery on the edge of town there, to yuh right. Hold yuh outfit there 'til I give the word. Me, I'm goin' straight in. This wagon, coupla boys, coupla gals. You bring the rest. I figure the gold shipment mebbe an hour behind us. We let it into town, right in there, then we close the net, do what we come all this way to do and start plannin' the future. Yessir! Yuh got all that, Goose? It clear enough for yuh?'

'I got it,' sighed Goose, 'but I still reckon—'

'Reckon not, my good friend!' smiled Ratrap, collecting the reins. 'Boys'll be here soon with the good news of all the killin' they done, gold's on its way, first president's waitin', Jerusalem beckons! God's in His Heaven and all's well with the world!'

'Amen,' groaned Goose.

Sam Cavendish eased his aching body to the soft comfort of the baled straw, released a long, exhausted sigh, and closed his eyes.

Hell, it would take no more than seconds for him to drift into sleep. Just that, only a few, peaceful, empty seconds. . . . He blinked into life again, rubbed his eyes, pushed himself clear of the bales and crossed to the shadowed side of the open livery doors.

He waited a moment before risking a quick glance to the right, to the silent, deserted main street into town, then to the left and the dust-bowl sprawl of sand and dirt to where, no more than stark grey shapes in the far distance, Ratrap's wagons were drawn up.

Good. Just as he wanted, he thought, easing back to the shadow. And with time to spare. He sighed again and relaxed. This was going to have to work, first time, no messing. No second chance. If anybody put so much as a boot wrong. . . .

Damn it, this was no time to get a twinge of doubt. It had to work it was all he had! He grunted and gazed into the high, cloudless, sunlit sky. Almost noon. Sheriff Church should have made it to the shipment wagons by now and halted them. 'Yuh'll stay with 'em, mister,' he had ordered as they had slowed their mounts at the approach to the Nagaro trail. 'Don't let 'em outa yuh sight and don't bring 'em within a sniff of town 'til yuh hear from me. I'll send somebody – always assumin' I can.'

'And just how the hell do yuh figure on stoppin' Ratrap, handlin' things in town, *alone*, f'Crissake, without—' Church had blustered.

'I'll think of somethin'. Damn it, I'll have to!'

Sure he would, he had pondered, after leaving the sheriff and riding the mare like the wind across the rougher, but shorter trail for Eldron, if only he had known where to begin!

He had slipped into town and made straight for O'Hara in the back room at the saloon.

'No time for long explanations,' he had told the bewildered proprietor. 'Sheriff talked with yuh this mornin', right? Right, so things are hummin' some and we ain't got a deal of time, so no questions, just do as I say. First, I want the livery far end of town to m'self. *Completely* to m'self, so get whoever owns it to clear out, but not before leavin' behind a box of dynamite. That's right, mister, dynamite! Second, I want this town closed down, quiet as the grave, not a soul in sight. Don't wanna hear so much as a breath. Do it anyhow, any way yuh like, only do it if yuh wanna stay in business. Right? Yuh understand?'

He had paused, blinked and steadied himself. 'The woman – Mrs Gates, she still here? She watchin' Clewes?'

'I ain't so sure who's doin' the watchin',' O'Hara had croaked. 'She's with him up there, in his room. No tellin' what—'

'Don't fret none, mister, she can handle herself.'

She was going to have to do just that, he had thought later as he left the saloon and slid away to the livery.

All quiet now, though, thought Cavendish, risking another glance. O'Hara had done a sound job, and if Ellie Gates was . . . best not think about her, not yet, not until this day had taken a deal more of its course. Not until them wagons out there were moving.

Twenty minutes later, Moses Ratrap was heading for town.

Twenty

Dirt shifted sullenly at the scuff of ponderous hoofs; wheels turned achingly, creaking like old arthritic joints under the weight they supported; worn and splintered timbers, drained and dry from the scorching sun, protested; leather strained, tack jangled, and the wagon came on slowly, grey and cracked as a shrivelled slug seeking shade.

Moses Ratrap was in no hurry, thought Cavendish, watching from the hatch to the loft above the livery, but that was not to say he was sitting there in a dozing stupor. You could bet your life there was not so much as a shadow out of place that missed his eagle gaze, not a sound he did not hear and interpret. And back of him, under the cover of canvas, guns at the ready, would be a handful of sidekicks just itching for the chance of a target.

Let him pass, decided Cavendish; let him get to the heart of town. Handling him there would be

143

no picnic, but the odds might just stand in favour of surprise, more so if there was no Goose Farrars leaping from the old man's shadow.

Cavendish swung his gaze to the second wagon. Farrars had the reins, a man at his side, the rest of the family back of him. He was in no hurry either. So maybe the plan was for Goose to take up station out of town, wait for the shipment outfits to break the horizon.

He grunted. That will do just fine, mister, he mused, his fingers idling over the box at his side. You just settle that wagon right there side of the livery stabling, right where I can see you – and blow you to Kingdom Come!

His gaze came back to Ratrap. Almost here now, still at the same pace, same steady grind, no thought of reining up in the scumbag's mind at the silence, the emptiness of the place. Hell, he must have noticed by now, thought the marshal, must be wondering how it was the town was so deserted. Maybe he figured this to be some planned reception, courtesy of the Eastern Federal!

Only minutes now before he passed and Farrars followed into position, fifteen at the outside and it would be the moment to ease the first of the dynamite from its bed in the box and put it to use, blast the first sticks short to spook the outfit's team, scatter the family from the canvas and set Goose running in circles.

He was reckoning on Ratrap's girls making a dash for it – they would have no stomach for a stand-off facing dynamite – to leave only Farrars and his men to face it out. Well, he might get lucky with his Winchester, but the hope lay in destruction – of Eldron, the whole damned town, if need be!

Cavendish grunted again as Ratrap's wagon passed beneath the livery hatch. He was almost tempted to raise his hat and bid the sonofabitch good morning! Instead, he began to sweat, ice-cold sweat, that clung in his neck, stung his back, slid like needles over his body.

Only his fingers, resting on the box, stayed dry and steady.

'Well, now, this is all very . . . very entertaining, my dear, but time has come—'

'Yuh stayin' right where yuh are, mister, for just as long as it suits,' smiled Ellie Gates turning from the window of the room and coming to the foot of the bed. 'I feel a whole lot safer with yuh trussed like that. Comfortable?'

'You—' spluttered Brenton Clewes, tugging at the cord binding his hands to the head of the bed while his body squirmed uselessly across the mattress. 'You two-timin', double-crossin' bitch! When I get my hands on you—'

'No chance,' said Ellie, folding her arms tightly. 'Not a hope in hell, mister. Yuh played along with

145

me, walked right into the web – slithered more like – and that's just where yuh stayin'. All yuh own doin'. Nobody else to blame. Me – I only did what was asked of me. Pretty well, it seems!'

'Asked?' blustered Clewes, squirming again. 'What do you mean, *asked*? Who asked you? Asked what?'

'Marshal Sam Cavendish. Lawman. Right here in town, mister, and all set to blow yuh schemin' gold heist sky-high! Him and me been sittin' on Moses Ratrap's tail for days.' Ellie's smile softened to a hard set of her lips. 'It's a long story and I ain't for tellin' it. All I'm interested in right now is makin' certain that sonofabitch gets what's comin' to him, and that you, Mister-first-president Brenton Clewes—'

'Hold on there, ma'am,' said Clewes, suddenly still on the bed, his gaze tight on Ellie's face, a softer, smoother edge to his voice. 'We should mebbe get to talkin' this through some. I don't see that you and me have a deal to fall out about. Fact, we could both be coming out of this to the good, don't you reckon?'

Ellie's folded arms stiffened across her breasts as she sighed, grunted and grinned gently. 'Well, now,' she mocked, 'yuh goin' to proposition me, Mr Clewes? Again! Hell, a woman my age never had it so good!'

'You could have it even better, ma'am.' Clewes winced at the bite of the cord. 'Figure it: you and

146

me together with all that gold. Could be done, ma'am. Oh, yes, could be done. I mean, that fellow Ratrap don't mean nothing. Just a scumbag. Now, if we were to take care of him – and I reckon we could – then turn our attentions to the lawman . . . why, the world and a fortune could be ours for the taking. I can be very generous, my dear. Very generous. And don't forget, that gold is mine. Oh, yes, all mine. My responsibility, the whole darned shipment. So what say we get together, eh? Pool our resources? Damn it, we were getting on well enough 'til—'

'Yuh mean, yuh *thought* we were,' smiled Ellie. 'Keen enough to get me up here, weren't yuh? Anxious enough to indulge y'self. Should never have let me tie yuh up like that, Mr Clewes. Bad judgement. No, yuh might be a first president when it comes to bankin', but yuh sure as hell two bits short of a supper when it comes to women! So I guess yuh know what yuh can do with yuh proposition. Yuh can go—'

Ellie's arms fell to her sides at the vicious roar and searing blast of an explosion. The window shook, glass panes cracked, splintered, clattered to the floor in gleaming silver shards. Clewes shuddered and began to sweat. A second blast seemed to thrust directly at the walls of the room, threatening to buckle every last plank of the cladding.

Ellie bit her lip, tossed her hair to her neck and

stumbled to the shattered window. She smiled at
the sight of licking flame and billowing smoke far
end of the street. Sam Cavendish at work! But the
smile faded and a chill twisted down her spine at
the closer sight of Moses Ratrap seated aboard his
wagon – right there in the street facing the
saloon, his gaze fixed like a rattler's stare on the
window, one hand resting on the Bible-box.

And, damn it, he had seen her!

Sam Cavendish flicked the hot sweat from his
face, took a firm grip on the Winchester and
spared himself a moment to take in his efforts.

It had worked, sure enough. Like hell it had!

The first sticks of dynamite thrown from the
loft hatch had halted Goose Farrars's outfit in its
tracks. Girls had screamed and tumbled like a
scattering of blown paper from the back of the
wagon and slithered for whatever cover was to
hand.

Farrars had reined the wagon team tight,
brought it under control and swung the outfit into
the livery corral, barking his orders to the men as
wheels ground to a halt and hoofs pounded dirt.

'Scatter!' he had yelled. 'Get y'selves hid!'

Cavendish's rifle had roared at the first targets.
He saw two men fall instantly, another squirm
away grasping his thigh. Farrars buried himself
beneath the wagon, his eyes swinging like lights
to pinpoint the marksman.

It took Goose only seconds to realize he had only single fire power ranged against him and less than a half-minute for that probing gaze to settle on the hatch.

But by then Cavendish had been on the move, dragging the box of dynamite from the hatch space into deeper shadow, selecting a handful of sticks and racing at full stretch for the stairway to the ground.

Ratrap's girls were staying put, too bewildered now to dare to move. Farrars and his men had regrouped then fanned out to approach the livery through a blaze of ripping, snarling lead.

So fire away, boys, the marshal had thought, you got nothing to shoot at!

Cavendish had waited a long minute before planting the next string of dynamite, this time in a tossed line covering the width of the street. The explosions, ripping out of the dirt like demons' tongues, had thrown Farrars's men in a slithering panic, but not before a hail of stray shots had penetrated the livery to explode the remaining dynamite in a whirling, twirling, swishing rush of fire, timber torn to matchwood and straw bales raging flame.

The smoke had been the marshal's cover to scoot deeper into town, firing at random at whatever offered as a target, but uncertain now where Farrars had holed-up and how soon he would follow.

He flicked another lathering of sweat to the dirt and slid away to the shadowed boardwalk. Only one way to head now: towards Ratrap. He could only guess at how long the inferno at the livery would occupy Farrars and hold him up. What the hell, the deck had been dealt – including the joker!

A few steps later and he had Ratrap's wagon in view. Only trouble was, its owner had disappeared.

Twenty-One

'You just get me outa this, Moses, d'yuh hear? Get me out right now, or so help me I'll—' Brenton Clewes squirmed like a trussed lizard on the bed, glared at Ellie Gates then at the grinning, dust-caked bulk of Ratrap framed in the open door, a Winchester cradled in his arms, the barrel stiff against Ellie's thigh. 'You hearin' me, Moses?'

'Oh, I'm hearin' yuh, Brenton, loud and clear I am,' drawled Ratrap, the grin spreading wet and loose. 'And I'm sure as hell seein' yuh! What a sight at that. Why, I never took a fine, upstandin' fella of the high-financin' type like y'self for indulgin' in such practices. That I did not.'

'T'ain't like you're seeing it,' moaned Clewes. 'Just untie me, will yuh?'

'Well, now, that all depends on whether the lady here is all through with yuh, don't it?' Ratrap freed a hand from the rifle to push at the brim of the floppy hat. 'Nice to see yuh again, ma'am. Real survivor, ain't yuh?' He spat over the carpet. 'Yuh

151

all done with him, lady, or gettin' started?'

'Moses, will you just do as I say, for God's sake?' spluttered Clewes. 'Don't you realize what's going on here? Can't yuh *see*, damn it? If we don't do somethin' soon, and very fast, there ain't goin' to be no gold, no nothin'. Now move!'

'Way now, steady up there.' Ratrap prodded the rifle deeper into Ellie's thigh. 'I just get the feelin' I ain't fully in the picture here. That so, lady? You folk holdin' out on me? Why, I roll peacefully into town and what do I find? Darn it, there ain't nothin' but mayhem aboundin' just everywhere. So what I wanna know—'

'The hell there's mayhem,' croaked Clewes, squirming again. 'I'll tell you what there is here – there's somebody blowin' the town apart, who's probably got to the shipment, and for all I know has a whole posse of lawmen ridin' in right now – and he, Moses, *is* the law! Marshal Sam Cavendish!'

Ellie shuddered at the bite of the barrel, the twitch of Ratrap's arms, the sudden surge of stale odour as the man broke to a streaky lathering of sweat.

'Him,' snarled Ratrap. 'That sonofabitch. Might have known.'

'You *know* him?' moaned Clewes. 'You mean to say you've been trailin' that Drift for nothin', with him sittin' on your tail, and this bitch along of him? Damn it, you ain't fit to lay a finger on my

152

gold! You're no better that a two-bit—'

'Shut it!' snapped Ratrap. 'I'll do the thinkin' from here on, and the one person who ain't touchin' that gold is you, mister. In fact, yuh ain't goin' no place. You're stayin' right here.' He spat again, then turned his slow, sullen gaze on Ellie. 'And you, lady, are goin' to be right alongside him, trussed to that bed like you and he were close as love ticks in a nest. Right there 'til I'm all through with this town and that gold's safely stowed.' He glared at Clewes again. 'Then, Mr Banker-man I'll get to showin' yuh who's two-bits when I come to cut yuh guts out. And I'll also show yuh before yuh bleed to death just how to handle this schemin'-eyed woman!'

It was then that Ellie Gates moved with all the speed and venom of a trapped viper.

She grabbed the rifle barrel and with all the strength she could summon pushed it high and to one side catching Ratrap unprepared and off balance. He stumbled against the bed, was blinded for a moment as the brim of his floppy hat covered his eyes and could only reach wildly for a hold on Ellie as she stumbled from the room to the landing and crashed towards the stairs.

She could hear Ratrap's curses, the thud of his steps pounding after her, knew then that there would be no hesitation once he had her in his sights. This time there would be no taking her alive, holding her for some future 'entertainment';

this time the Winchester would rage with only killing in mind.

She was halfway down the stairs, sliding along the side of the banister, when a roaring volley of shots from the street startled her to a plunge to her right. The banister creaked, began to split under her weight and seconds later collapsed as Ratrap loomed like a shadow above her.

His shot blazed into the space where Ellie had stood, shattered a hanging lantern, whined and ricocheted into the bar and buried the lead in a wall. Ellie crashed out of view, arms and legs in a spinning tumble, felt herself thud against a table, roll clear of it to scatter chairs, coughed, spluttered, began to choke and was only half aware of where she was when a hand grabbed her by the shoulder and hoisted her into the darkness.

'Get y'self into real trouble if yuh not careful, ma'am,' muttered O'Hara dragging Ellie into the back room and closing the door softly behind him. He smiled and placed a finger to his lips. 'Not a sound,' he hissed.

The shots beyond the batwings had diverted Ratrap from the hunt, halting him on the stairs, the rifle probing ahead of him, his body tensed, eyes glinting in a narrowed gaze. He spat at the sounds of Clewes's protests from the room, waited a moment, glanced at the broken banister and came on.

It took him a full minute to reach the foot of the

stairs, cross the deserted bar and sidle to the window fronting the street. He licked his lips at the sight of the two bodies sprawled in the dirt: his men, dead as stone, and no need to guess at whose hand. He spat again. 'Sonofabitch!' he murmured, and slid towards the batwings.

He waited, watching, narrowing his gaze over his empty wagon. Where the hell was Goose and the others? Where were the townsfolk? Where was the gold? But right now, just where was Sam Cavendish?

Ratrap eased the 'wings open, passed through them to the boardwalk, paused, flicked an eye to the pall of thick smoke from the livery, and eased into the street, the Winchester fanning over space and silence.

He scuffed dirt, step by careful step, closing on the wagon, watching for the slightest movement. Damn that woman, he cursed. Damn that first president. Rot in hell, the pair of them. But maybe there was still time to get to that shipment once Goose showed up and they got organized. Once that trailing lawman was off his back. . . .

Ratrap reached the wagon, murmured softly to the wild-eyed team, climbed slowly, carefully aboard and into the drive seat. All it needed now was steady thinking, a clear uncluttered head.

He was reaching with one hand for a hold on the reins when the single shot from the shadowed boardwalk spun the rifle clear of his grip to the ground. He cursed, hissed, wrung his hand and glared like a starved hound at the sight of Cavendish stepping into the street, his levelled Winchester glinting in the sun's glare.

'That's it, Moses,' clipped the marshal. 'It's over. Yuh all through.'

'Damn me if it ain't Sam Cavendish,' grinned Ratrap. 'Who'd have reckoned it? All this time, all this way. Why, I do indeed congratulate yuh, Marshal. Real impressive. Good Lord must be walkin' at yuh side.'

'He ain't nowhere near yours,' snapped Cavendish. 'Given yuh up like rotten meat, so you just step down from that outfit there real easy and get y'self ready for a hangin'. Get yuh a preacher if there's the time – which I doubt! Now move!'

'Gotta hand it to yuh, Marshal, you are a persistent sonofabitch, and no mistake,' said Ratrap spreading his arms wide. 'Don't know how yuh done all this, but yuh sure as hell made some snatch here.' He lowered his arms, one hand coming to rest on the Bible-box. 'And I guess the Good Lord has a few words fittin' for an occasion like this. Sure to have. So mebbe yuh'll just spare me the time to take a look here, eh, see what the Good Book has to say?' Ratrap's fingers spread like a claw over the cover. 'Now—'

'*Sam! The box!*'

The shout came from the saloon as Ellie Gates

crashed through the batwings to the boardwalk.

'*The Bible! It ain't*—'

Cavendish half turned to Ellie, was caught for a moment between her and Ratrap, was suddenly sweating, his grip hot and tight on the rifle, then turning again to the wagon as Ratrap's hand came clear of the open box, the Colt levelled like a tongue of flame.

'Good Lord always has the last word,' grinned Ratrap. 'Always!'

'Too right!' said Cavendish, and let go a raging roar of fire from the rifle where it hugged his hip.

Ratrap's gun flew clear, his arms spread like crumpled wings, the floppy hat spun to the ground, his eyes glazed in a flat, defiant stare and his grin froze to a twisted crease across his lips as he hit the dirt in a blood-soaked sprawl.

'Stand clear! Get away!' yelled Cavendish at the sound of hoofbeats through the smoke cloud over the livery. Farrars! It could only be Goose making one last—

'Hold yuh fire, Marshal. Yuh done enough for one day!'

Sheriff Church reined his mount to a slithering halt, holstered his Colt, tipped his hat and sat easy in the saddle.

'Well, yuh didn't really figure me for missin' out on all the action, did yuh?' he said smiling into the marshal's sweating face. 'Shipment's safe just outa town. Some of the company boys helped me clear up Farrars and his scum. Don't seem a deal more to be done, does there?'

They turned to the saloon and lifted their gazes to the angry curses from an upstairs room.

'Somebody seems a mite distressed,' grinned Cavendish. 'All yours, Mr Church. All yours!'

Sam Cavendish lounged idly in the shadows of the boardwalk at the Eldron Mercantile and watched in silence as Ellie Gates put the finishing touches to the packs roped to the mount alongside her saddled horse.

She seemed determined enough, he thought. Had the look of a woman with her mind made up and not for changing it. Pity. Another couple of days and—

'Yuh can look on long as yuh like, Marshal,' called Ellie without turning, 'but won't do no good. You got your life, I got mine. Mine's out there, straight down that trail, far West as it goes.' She tugged defiantly at a rope. 'And don't give me that "rough-country, wild-men, maraudin'-Indians" talk. Don't give a damn! After this – *all* this, every last sonofabitch drop of it – I'm out. Right out. Got me a horse, got me a pack, rifle, food, water, clean clothes and a trail map – sorta – and that'll do.'

She tugged again, relaxed and stared into empty space. 'It's over,' she said quietly. 'All done.

Wichita marshal ridin' in to settle Clewes, Sheriff Church here gettin' the town back to shape. Gold company happy, bank happy. Y'self headin' back East, I suppose. Well, not for me. Back East is no place. Don't exist. Too many bad memories. Too much lost.' She brushed at a sudden tear, then tossed her pony-tail hair into her neck. 'No, it's West for me and that's that. And I ain't troubled about travellin' alone. Anybody who can handle the Drift, Ratrap, Apaches. . . . Well, it don't matter none, does it? I'm goin! Noon. No messin'. And I thank yuh kindly for all yuh done. Real grateful.'

She was silent for a moment. 'Yuh goin' to say somethin', Sam Cavendish, or just stand there starin'?' she added without turning.

'Starin's just fine, ma'am,' murmured Cavendish.

Ellie swung round. 'So what yuh starin' at?' she snapped.

'You, ma'am. Just admirin'. Thinkin' on how I'm goin' to miss havin' that pretty butt around.'

'Mr Cavendish! Yuh gettin' a mite above y'self, ain't yuh? I'm not sure I wanna hear that sorta talk. T'ain't fittin'.'

'No, ma'am, yuh right, it ain't. Not one bit fittin'. True enough – but not fittin'.' Cavendish stepped casually from the shadows. 'Join me in a drink before yuh go? Saloon in ten minutes?'

Ellie Gates stamped her foot in the dirt as she

watched the marshal stroll away. 'Pretty butt, my hat!' she pouted, then smiled softly to herself. 'Well – and why not? Damn it, why not!'